CANVAS OF SECRETS

PHILLIP DAIGLE

PLAN B

SECOND EDITION

*For Gisela, my life's compass
and my life's greatest story.*

PRAISE FOR THE AUTHOR

A satisfying mystery filled with intriguing characters.

Ray Stone, formerly of the LAPD (until he blew his cover during a major sting operation), is biding his time in California's sleepy, artsy town of Laguna Beach. He misses the adrenaline-fueled high-octane police work of Los Angeles and is waiting for a chance to redeem himself.

Early in the morning on New Year's Day, 1969, a call comes in from dispatch: "Dead body at Shaw's Cove." The victim is Amelia Hart, a wealthy 50-something member of the artistic community and an anti-war activist. Her body is badly bruised. The officer on the scene says it is a suicide, but Ray suspects there is more to the story.

Meanwhile, Dennis Driver, a reporter with the local Daily Pilot and a Vietnam War veteran, is battling depression and PTSD-like symptoms. On New Year's Day, he checks the newspaper and sees that his story had been scrapped for one written by a more experienced reporter. When he dejectedly enters the newsroom, his editor hands him an opportunity for his big break: Report on the suspicious death of Amelia Hart.

As Ray and Dennis, working separately but occasionally sharing information, begin digging into the secrets hidden behind the glossy facade of Amelia's life, they lead readers through the dark underbelly of the high-priced art world.

The twisty, methodically paced narrative is as much a character study of two men struggling to overcome their inner demons and begin anew as it is an engaging mystery.

KIRKUS REVIEWS

CONTENTS

1. Amelia's Last Party — 1
2. The Morning After — 6
3. Cold Tides — 10
4. A Story That Matters — 17
5. Difficult Truths — 22
6. Without Amelia — 28
7. Beauty and Grief — 34
8. The Dealer — 40
9. Wounds and Clues — 46
10. Nothing to Hide — 51
11. The Heir Apparent — 57
12. Thirty Days — 61
13. Gated and Guarded — 65
14. Oil and Motive — 70
15. Persons of Interest — 76
16. The Monet in the Closet — 84
17. Portraits and Politics — 89
18. Political Art — 94
19. Erasing the Artist — 101
20. Bigger than a Byline — 105
21. The Note — 108
22. Debt and Motive — 112
23. Something to Protect — 115
24. The Confidence Game — 119
25. The Farm and the Facade — 123
26. The Battle after the War — 128
27. Out of the System — 134
28. A Beautiful Lie — 138
29. Beyond the Self — 143
30. The Interview — 148
31. The Weight We Carry — 153
32. Ghosts and Suspects — 157

33. What We Don't Say   161
34. Almost Too Good to be True   166
35. Patriots and Pretenders   171
36. Painted into a Corner   179
37. The Right to Remain Silent   187
38. A House Made Whole   193
39. Echoes from the Bluff   200
40. Freedom, Signed in Ink   208
41. The Artist and the Debt   213
42. Beneath the Surface   219
43. No Going Back   228
44. Provenance   234
45. Proof of Intent   240
46. The Final Brush Stroke   247
    Epilogue   255

Also by Phillip Daigle   257
About the Author   259

1. AMELIA'S LAST PARTY

New Year's Eve 1968

Amelia Hart stood at her living room window, watching the light change over the Pacific. The ocean stretched endlessly toward the horizon, its surface catching the last amber rays of the year's final day. She held a glass of wine—her second, though she rarely counted anymore—and considered the placement of her paintings in the shifting light.

The Wendt landscape dominated the far wall, all bold strokes and California optimism. Across from it, the Cuprien seemed to argue for a different vision of the coast, more introspective, more aware of shadows. She'd moved the small Hinkle still life three times today, finally settling it on the mantel where it could exist peacefully between the larger works.

"Mom, have you seen my suede jacket?"

Julie appeared in the doorway, her blonde hair loose around her shoulders, wearing a cream sweater and bellbottoms that flared dramatically at the ankles. At twenty-three, she moved through the world with the particular confidence of her generation—unencumbered by the careful considerations that had shaped Amelia's youth.

"Try the hall closet," Amelia said, then noticed what her daughter wasn't wearing. "Julie, are you planning to go out like that?"

"Like what?" Julie tilted her head, genuinely puzzled.

"Without a bra. People will notice."

Julie's laugh was bright and uncomplicated. "Oh, Mom. It's 1969. Nobody cares about that anymore." She disappeared toward the hallway, her voice floating back. "Besides, I'm wearing the jacket."

Amelia found herself remembering her own mother's voice from thirty years ago: *A lady never leaves the house without proper foundation garments, Amelia.* She'd worn a girdle to her wedding, gloves to church every Sunday, stockings even in summer heat. When had the world decided to shed all that careful construction?

Julie returned, pulling on the brown suede jacket, adjusting the silver peace sign that hung from a thin chain around her neck—a gift from some boy Amelia had never met, whose name Julie mentioned less and less lately.

"Where are you going tonight?" Amelia asked.

"The Golden Bear in Huntington Beach. There's a band from Los Angeles—the Doors."

"Unusual name."

"Cathy's driving, and Becky's coming." Julie checked her reflection in the hall mirror, tucking her hair behind her ears in the same unconscious gesture she'd had since childhood. "You know Becky—the sweet one you're always going on about."

Amelia did know Becky, had watched both girls grow from awkward teenagers into young women with strong opinions about everything—except what they wanted to do with their lives. Julie had been drifting since college, taking photography classes, working part-time at the gallery, dating boys who seemed to disappear as quickly as they'd arrived.

"When will you be home?" Amelia asked.

"Late. They don't even start playing until after eleven." Julie turned from the mirror, her expression softening slightly. "I'm not sixteen anymore, Mom."

"I know." Amelia moved closer, catching the faint scent of patchouli that seemed to follow her daughter everywhere these days. "I just thought you might want to ring in the New Year here. With me. Like we used to."

"The show won't be over until well past midnight." Julie leaned in and kissed Amelia's cheek, lingering for just a moment longer than usual.

Amelia watched from the window as Julie climbed into Cathy's Volkswagen van, her blonde hair catching the porch light before the van pulled away down the coastal highway. The taillights disappeared around the curve, and Amelia stood there longer than necessary, as if waiting might somehow bring them back.

The catering staff arrived at seven, their efficiency transforming the house into something ready for celebration. Amelia changed into a black cocktail dress.

By eight-thirty, her friends filled the rooms with conversation and laughter.

Amelia moved through her living room, champagne flute in hand, nodding at Dr. Reynolds and his wife as they admired the Wendt. The Hendersons from next door clustered near the fireplace, Margaret's diamond earrings catching the light as she gestured toward the Hinkle still life. The usual crowd—

comfortable, predictable, with their sensible haircuts and carefully considered opinions on brushwork and provenance.

"Magnificent gathering, Amelia." Charles Whitfield appeared at her elbow, immaculate in his navy blazer. He'd been collecting California impressionists since before it became fashionable. "That new Cuprien is absolute perfection in this light."

"Thank you, Charles." She smiled, watching Diane Porter across the room, her salt-and-pepper bob swinging as she leaned in to examine the painting's corner signature.

"Amelia, this place never stops being magnificent," Patricia said, joining her by the ocean-facing windows. "Is

Julie joining us?"

"She's at a concert with friends." Amelia straightened a champagne flute on the side table, avoiding Patricia's knowing look. "You know how young people are."

By 1:30 am, all of her guests were gone. Amelia changed into her navy blue swimsuit, the practical one-piece she preferred for her nightly routine. She wrapped herself in a thick terrycloth robe and stepped outside. The January air carried a chill, but the heated pool sent wisps of steam into the night, a ghostly invitation.

The world tilted slightly as Amelia shed her robe and placed it on the deck chair. She hadn't meant to drink so much, but every time her glass emptied, someone had filled it.

Her foot tested the water. Perfect. The pool heater hummed efficiently in the darkness, maintaining the temperature she preferred regardless of the season. Amelia slipped in with barely a splash, the warm water enveloping her like a second skin.

The first few strokes felt clumsy, her limbs uncoordinated. The wine had dulled her senses more than she'd realized. But muscle memory took over as she pushed through the water. One lap. Two. Her breathing found its rhythm.

The voice came between strokes.

Amelia faltered mid-lap, treading water as she listened. Perhaps it was just the wind, or distant traffic on the coastal highway. But there it came again—voices. The words were too indistinct to make out.

She swam to the edge of the pool, water streaming from her hair as she lifted herself to listen. The sound seemed to come from the point.

"Hello?" she called, her voice sounding thin in the vast night.

2. THE MORNING AFTER

Ray Stone had chosen Laguna Beach the way some people choose exile—deliberately, but not without regret. Four months ago, he'd been Detective Ray Stone of the LAPD. Now he was simply Ray Stone, the lone investigator for a coastal town where the most serious crimes usually involved stolen surfboards or gallery break-ins.

He sat in the Renaissance Bakery on New Year's morning, nursing his second cup of coffee and watching the town wake up through salt-stained windows. The locals moved with the unhurried pace of people who lived where others vacationed. Artists carried easels toward the bluffs. Shop owners swept sidewalks clean of sand and celebration debris from the night before.

The coffee was stronger here than in Los Angeles, and the silence was something he was still learning to appreciate. Back in the city, quiet meant trouble. Here, it simply meant morning—though Ray had begun to suspect he might never fully trust quiet again.

It had been six months since the Ramirez case went sideways. Six months since his testimony at the corruption hearing, when he'd watched three fellow detectives get indicted and his own career effectively end. They'd called him a whistleblower in the newspapers. His partner had called him other things before requesting a transfer and never speaking to him again.

Ray had grown up forty miles inland, where the air tasted of exhaust and ambition. Laguna's salt-sweet atmosphere still felt foreign, like wearing clothes that didn't quite fit. He'd thought about leaving—going back east, maybe, starting over somewhere that didn't remind him daily of the career he'd left behind. But something about the constancy of the ocean kept him anchored, even when he wasn't sure he wanted to be.

His apartment overlooked Wood's Cove, a small crescent of beach tucked between rocky outcroppings. He'd taken to walking there at dawn, watching the light change on the water. It was better than the insomnia that had plagued him in Los Angeles, where sleep came in fragments between emergency calls and the weight of what he'd seen.

The phone booth outside the bakery rang, its shrill tone cutting through the morning quiet. Ray watched a teenager answer it, then hang up and continue walking. Different world, he thought. In the city, a ringing phone always meant urgency—usually someone else's tragedy becoming your responsibility.

He finished his coffee and left exact change on the table—a habit from ten years of grabbing meals between calls. The walk back to his apartment took him past galleries still closed for the holiday, their windows displaying paintings of the very coastline he now called home.

Main Beach was nearly empty, just a few early joggers and an old man walking his dog near the tide line. The usual New Year's Day casualties—teenagers sleeping off hangovers in their cars, couples walking slowly with sunglasses despite the overcast sky. Normal enough, but something felt slightly off-kilter, the way a room looks different when someone has moved all the furniture two inches to the left.

Ray told himself it was just the holiday quiet, the way coastal towns held their breath the morning after the celebration. But fifteen years of police work had taught him to pay attention to that feeling, even when—especially when—he couldn't identify its source.

The ocean was flat and gray under the overcast sky, its surface broken only by the occasional pelican diving for fish. Ray had tried surfing twice since moving here—a concession to starting over—but the ocean seemed to require a patience he hadn't yet developed. The waves moved according to their own logic, indifferent to human schedules or expectations. Maybe that was what he needed to learn.

B ack in his apartment, Ray made fresh coffee and settled at the small table by the window. He'd been reading Steinbeck lately—something about the California coast felt appropriate—and the book lay open to a passage about the sea's ability to heal. He wasn't sure he believed it yet, but he was willing to find out.

From his window, he could see Wood's Cove clearly, the small beach where he'd walked just an hour earlier. The tide was coming in, waves washing higher up the sand with each cycle. In a few hours, the beach would be crowded with families, kids building sandcastles, and teenagers playing volleyball. The normal rhythms of life that had somehow eluded him for months.

The phone rang at 7:00 AM.

"Ray? It's dispatch. We've got a situation at Shaw's Cove. Body on the rocks. Looks suspicious."

Ray set down his coffee cup and reached for his jacket, already feeling the familiar weight of responsibility settling on his shoulders. Through the window, he could see the rocks below, still peaceful in the morning light, giving no hint of what waited there.

"I'll be right there."

As he walked down the coastal path toward the beach, Ray felt something shift inside him—not quite readiness, but recognition. For four months, he'd been a man without a real purpose, floating between his old life and whatever came next. Now, suddenly, he was a detective again.

The morning air carried the scent of kelp and salt, and somewhere in the distance, a foghorn sounded its low, mournful note. Whatever waited for him on those rocks would pull him back into the world he'd tried to leave behind. But perhaps, Ray thought as his footsteps quickened on the path, that had always been inevitable.

The ocean kept its own schedule, and it had just delivered something that would change everything—again.

3. COLD TIDES

The morning mist clung to Shaw's Cove like a shroud, turning the familiar beach into something strange and unwelcoming. Ray had walked this path since moving to Laguna Beach, but never to examine a body. As he descended toward the yellow tape and clustered uniforms, he felt the familiar tightness in his chest—part adrenaline, part dread. In Los Angeles, dead bodies had been statistics. Here, they were neighbors.

The scene below was carefully orchestrated chaos—paramedics packing equipment, uniformed officers maintaining a perimeter, and the orange-jacketed lifeguards who had pulled Amelia Hart from the rocks looking like they wished they were anywhere else. Someone had covered her with a yellow tarp, but the ocean had already told most of its story in the arrangement of her limbs, the torn fabric of her swimsuit, the way the morning light caught the water still dripping from her gray hair.

Ray approached the body with the methodical pace he'd learned in fifteen years of police work. This was the moment that mattered most—the first look, before assumptions hardened into conclusions. Before politics and convenience started writing the report.

Sergeant O'Neil appeared at his elbow, clipboard in hand and impatience radiating from every gesture. "Waste of your time coming down here, Stone. Clear-cut suicide. Woman takes a header off the cliff, ocean does the rest." O'Neil had been with Laguna Beach PD for twenty years and had the territorial instincts of a bulldog. He treated Ray's LAPD experience like a communicable disease.

Ray crouched beside the body without responding, pulling back the tarp with practiced care. Amelia Hart had been a handsome woman, probably in her early fifties, with the kind of careful grooming that spoke of money and social position. The navy-blue swimsuit was practical rather than fashionable —a swimmer's suit, not a sunbather's. But it was torn in several places, and the damage told conflicting stories. The left shoulder strap was nearly severed, as if yanked rather than scraped. Fabric bunched at the waist suggested grabbing hands, not tumbling rocks.

Ray's pulse quickened—the old detective instincts awakening after months of dormancy. "Any witnesses?"

"Daughter found her this morning. Julie Bloom. Lives up in the main house." O'Neil gestured toward the cliff where a Mediterranean-style mansion perched like a white bird against the gray sky. "Says Mom went for her usual swim last night and never came back. Open and shut."

"Nothing's ever open and shut, O'Neil." The words came out sharper than Ray intended, carrying years of frustration with lazy police work. He softened his tone. "The daughter— she usually swam down here?"

O'Neil's mustache twitched with irritation. "That's the thing. Daughter says no. Says her mom always used the lap pool up at the house. Did thirty laps every night, regular as clockwork."

Ray looked from the body to the house, calculating angles and distances. The cold in his chest spread, familiar as an old wound. "Then what was she doing down here?"

"Maybe she changed her routine. Maybe she was drunk— they had a big party last night. Maybe she wanted to try something different before offing herself." O'Neil's tone suggested he'd already filed the case in his mind, stamped it closed, and moved on to easier problems.

Ray stood, brushing sand from his knees. A woman who swam thirty laps every night in her heated pool doesn't suddenly decide to swim in the ocean on a cold January evening. Not unless someone convinced her to. "Where's the daughter now?"

"Up at the house with some neighbor lady. Pretty broken up, as you'd expect. Though you never can tell with rich folks —they hide things different."

Ray took one more look around the cove, memorizing details the way his old partner had taught him: the angle of the rocks, the height of the tide, the way the morning light fell across the sand. By afternoon, this would be just another pretty beach where families spread blankets and children built sand-castles. The ocean was already working to forget what had happened here. But Ray wouldn't let it.

The path up to the house was steep and winding, carved into the cliff face with the kind of careful engineering that money could buy. Halfway up, Ray paused to catch his breath and look back down at the cove. From this height, the beach looked small, the rocks that had claimed Amelia Hart nothing more than dark points in the foam. Far enough to fall. Far enough to throw someone.

· · ·

A Young woman in her early twenties with blonde hair pulled back carelessly and eyes red from crying. She wore jeans and a USC sweatshirt that looked like it hadn't been changed since the night before. Her hands trembled as she gripped the door frame.

"Miss Bloom? Detective Ray Stone. I'm sorry for your loss."

She nodded jerkily, stepping aside to let him in. Coffee had spilled down the front of her sweatshirt—fresh stains over old ones. "Thank you. The other officer said—he said someone would need to ask questions. About Mom." Her voice caught on the last word.

The house's interior was elegant but lived-in, with the kind of art collection that took decades to assemble. Ray noticed several empty wine glasses scattered on side tables, and the lingering scent of cigarette smoke and perfume suggested the party had been well-attended. A champagne flute lay shattered near the fireplace, as if dropped and forgotten.

"Can you tell me about last night?" Ray asked gently, settling into a chair across from where Julie perched on the edge of a sofa like a bird ready to take flight.

"Mom had her New Year's Eve party. She does, did, one every year. About thirty people, I think." Julie's hands moved constantly—smoothing her hair, picking at her sleeves, reaching for tissues. "It went until after midnight. I went to a concert in Huntington Beach with friends. The Doors." The last detail emerged like a confession.

"What time did you get home?"

"Around two-thirty. Maybe three. I was…we were having fun, and I didn't want to come home to Mom's stuffy friends talking about art and dead painters." Guilt flooded her face.

"God, I'm horrible. She wanted me to stay for midnight, to ring in the New Year together, and I just…I left her alone."

"When did you realize something was wrong?"

Julie stood abruptly, began pacing to the window, and back. "This morning, around seven. I went to make coffee, and I was so hungover, and I dropped the pot, and it crashed, and I thought, 'Great, now I'll wake Mom up,' but she didn't come down to see what happened. She always came down." The words tumbled out faster now. "So, I cleaned up the mess and went looking for her, and I saw the sliding door to the pool was open. That's not like Mom. She always locked up at night, always. So I went outside, and I saw her robe by the pool chair.

Ray made notes, but his mind was working on the timeline, the logistics, the human element. "You said your mother always swam in the pool?"

"Every night. Thirty laps, no matter what. Even when it was raining, even when she was sick." Julie's voice gained strength when talking about her mother's routines. "She said it helped her think, helped her sleep. It was like… like meditation for her."

"But last night she went to the ocean instead."

"I don't understand it." Julie's composure cracked again. "Mom wouldn't swim in the ocean at night, especially alone, without a buddy.

Ray felt the pieces of the puzzle shifting, refusing to form the picture O'Neil wanted to see. Amelia Hart didn't suddenly decide to brave the ocean in January, especially in the wee hours. "I'd like to look around outside, if that's all right."

Julie nodded, then grabbed his arm as he stood. "Detective Stone? That other officer thinks Mom killed herself. But she wouldn't. She was sad sometimes, but she was planning things. People who are planning don't..."

"I'll keep an open mind," Ray promised, and meant it.

The pool area was pristine. Ray examined the deck carefully, looking for signs of struggle, drops of blood, anything that might suggest violence. The concrete had been hosed down recently; he could smell the chlorine evaporating in the morning sun. Someone had been thorough.

He walked to the edge of the property where a metal staircase led down to a small private beach. The stairs were steep and narrow, more like a fire escape than a proper path. Ray tested the handrail—solid, but slick with morning dew and something else. Oil, maybe, or lotion. It would be treacherous to navigate in the dark, especially for someone who had been drinking. Or someone who was being forced.

At the bottom, he found himself on a tiny crescent of sand, barely large enough for two people. The tide was higher now, lapping at rocks that would have been exposed the night before. Ray tried to imagine Amelia Hart making her way down these stairs in a swimsuit, in the dark, to swim in water she feared.

The image wouldn't come. But another one would: Amelia Hart being carried or thrown down these stairs, conscious or unconscious, by someone who knew the tides, who knew she'd be found in the morning, who wanted it to look like a suicide.

Back at the house, he found Julie in the kitchen, staring out the window at the pool with hollow eyes.

"Miss Bloom, I need to ask—did your mother have any enemies? Anyone who might have wanted to hurt her?"

Julie looked genuinely surprised. "Enemies? No, Mom

was... she was an artist and a collector who had dinner parties. Everyone loved her."

"What about money? Debts? Business problems?"

"No, nothing like that. My stepfather left her well provided for. The art collection alone is worth..." Julie stopped, a new thought occurring to her. "You really don't think she killed herself."

"I think your mother was murdered," Ray said simply. "And whoever did it wanted it to look like something else entirely."

Julie sank into a chair, the weight of this new reality settling on her shoulders. "But who would want to hurt Mom? And why?"

Ray left his card and walked back to his car, those questions echoing in his mind. By the time he reached the station, he was certain of three things: Amelia Hart didn't kill herself. She didn't drown by accident either. Someone had wanted her dead badly enough to plan it carefully, execute it cleanly, and cover it up professionally.

The question wasn't whether Amelia Hart had been murdered. The question was who had killed her, and what secret had died with her on the rocks of Shaw's Cove.

4. A STORY THAT MATTERS

Dennis Driver pulled into the Daily Pilot parking lot with Dylan's "Subterranean Homesick Blues" rattling his Volkswagen's speakers. Three months out of the Army, two months on the job, and still waiting for a story that matters. The newsroom reeked of coffee, cigarettes, typewriter ribbon, and something more abstract—deadline sweat. Dennis had grown to love that smell. It meant possibility, the chance that today might be the day he proved he belonged here.

He'd gotten the job partly because he was a veteran—the paper was running short on young reporters after the draft had claimed half the staff. His editor, EK Hornbeck, had served in Korea and understood what it meant to come home and try to build something from scratch.

Dennis settled at his desk and pulled out his story on the anti-war demonstration from the weekend. He'd spent two days on it, interviewing protesters and police, trying to capture the tension without taking sides. In Vietnam, he'd learned to watch and listen before making judgments. It seemed like a useful skill for journalism.

An hour later, he carried the finished piece to Janice, EK's secretary, who guarded the editor's office like a benevolent dragon.

"He's in a mood today," she warned, nodding toward EK's closed door. "Michael Torres got the front page again."

Dennis felt his stomach tighten. Michael had fifteen years' experience and connections throughout Orange County. Dennis had a high school typing class and three months of covering zoning meetings.

When EK finally called him in, the older man looked tired and was chewing antacids like candy. His desk was covered with photographs, page layouts, and half-empty coffee cups.

"Your demonstration piece," EK said without preamble, washing down a Tums with cold coffee. "Good reporting, solid interviews. But Michael's story had more context, better sources." He looked up at Dennis over his reading glasses. "Experience matters in this business. Sources take time to develop."

Dennis felt the heat rise in his face. "I spent two days on that story."

"And Michael spent two years building relationships with the police chief and the protest organizers. That's the difference." EK's voice wasn't unkind, but it was final. "When I was starting, I missed a big story—city hall corruption scandal—because I was too green to see what was right in front of me. Took me five years to live it down."

"Yes, sir." The words tasted like chalk.

EK studied him for a moment, then grimaced and popped another antacid. "This coffee's eating a hole in my stomach, like every rookie reporter I've ever hired. You're angry. That's not necessarily bad. Anger can fuel good journalism if you channel it right. But don't let it make you sloppy." He rifled through the papers on his desk. "Speaking of which, I might have something for you."

He pulled out a press release and tossed it across the desk. "Local woman found dead on the beach this morning. Amelia Hart, a wealthy widow, an artist, lived down in Laguna Beach. Police are calling it suicide, but the family's asking questions."

Dennis scanned the brief report. "What kind of questions?"

"The kind that make good stories. The daughter doesn't believe her mother killed herself.." EK leaned back in his chair. "Could be nothing, a loved one's denial."

Dennis felt something stir in his chest—the jungle-born instinct that said: this doesn't add up. "You want me to check it out?"

"I want you to talk to the family, talk to the cops, see if there's a story there. Real reporting, not just rewriting what comes over the wire." EK's expression softened slightly. "This is your chance to show me what you can do with a story that matters."

Dennis was already reaching for his jacket. "I'm on it."

Driving down the Pacific Coast Highway reminded Dennis why he'd stayed in California after his discharge. The ocean appeared and disappeared between hills, blue and endless under the January sky.

He'd found a room to let in Laguna Beach after getting out of the Army. It was the kind of place where artists and wealthy retirees lived side by side, where galleries sold paintings for more than most people made in a year. If Amelia Hart had been wealthy enough to collect art, her death would have mattered to people with influence.

The Laguna Beach Police Department was a small building

on Forest Avenue, designed to blend in with the town's artistic aesthetic. Dennis parked and checked his notebook, running through the questions he wanted to ask.

Inside, a desk sergeant with sun-weathered skin looked up from his paperwork. "Help you?"

"Dennis Driver, Daily Pilot. I'm looking for information about Amelia Hart—the woman found on the beach this morning."

The sergeant's expression closed off immediately. "You'll need to talk to Sergeant O'Neil. He's handling the case."

"Is he available?"

"He's at lunch. Try again this afternoon."

Dennis thanked him and walked back outside, frustrated but not surprised. Small-town police departments didn't like talking to reporters, especially about deaths that might generate unwanted attention.

D ennis found the Hart home perched on a cliff overlooking Shaw's Cove. The house was impressive— white stucco with a red tile roof, surrounded by carefully maintained gardens. A black Lincoln Continental sat in the circular driveway next to a newer Volkswagen van.

Dennis parked on the street and walked to the front door, notebook in hand. This was the part of journalism he was still learning—how to approach grieving families, how to ask painful questions without seeming like a vulture.

A young woman answered the door.

"Miss Hart? I'm Dennis Driver from the Daily Pilot. I'm very sorry for your loss."

She studied his face for a moment, her posture defensive.

"It's Miss Bloom, actually, Julie Bloom." Her voice was hoarse. "If this is about the paperwork or the insurance companies—"

"No, nothing like that. I was hoping you might be willing to talk about your mother. I understand you have some concerns about the circumstances of her death."

Julie looked past him toward the street, then back at his face. Something in his expression—maybe the weariness, maybe the steadiness—seemed to settle her. "You're not like the other reporters who called. You actually seem to care."

"I'd like to understand who she was, not just how she died."

She hesitated, then stepped aside. "Would you like to come in? I'll make coffee."

As Dennis followed her into the elegant house, he felt the familiar tingle of a story beginning to unfold. In Vietnam, he'd learned to trust his instincts about when something was wrong. Looking at this beautiful house, thinking about a woman who supposedly killed herself by swimming in water she feared, those same instincts were telling him that nothing about Amelia Hart's death was as simple as it appeared.

It was his chance to prove he belonged in journalism—by finding the truth that everyone else wanted to ignore.

5. DIFFICULT TRUTHS

Dennis knew Shaw's Cove well. He'd been renting a room just up the hill since his discharge three months ago, and the beach had become part of his morning routine, a way to clear his head before facing whatever the day brought.

This morning, the beach wasn't a refuge. It was a crime scene.

He parked on Cliff Drive and walked down the familiar path to the sand. The cove was sheltered between rocky outcroppings, popular with locals but hidden from the main tourist beaches. If Amelia Hart had swum here regularly, someone would have noticed.

Frisbee Norm was already on the beach, throwing his disc to himself with the practiced rhythm of someone who'd made this his daily meditation. Dennis had met him a few times—a former Wall Street trader who'd dropped out and moved to Laguna Beach to surf and throw frisbees. He was exactly the kind of person who'd know the beach regulars.

"Hey, Denny!" Norm called, tossing the frisbee in Dennis's direction. "Haven't seen you around lately."

Dennis caught the disc and threw it back. "Been working. New job at the Daily Pilot."

"No kidding? What kind of stories do you cover?"

"Right now, I'm working on one about Amelia Hart. The woman they found dead here yesterday morning." Dennis watched Norm's face carefully. "Did you know her?"

Norm's expression grew serious. "Yeah, I knew Amelia." He caught the frisbee but didn't throw it back.

"Heard they're calling it suicide." Dennis asked, "What do you think?"

Norm shook his head. "Doesn't make sense. Amelia was tough as nails." He gestured toward the water. "She'd swim straight across the mouth of the cove and back. That takes serious mental strength."

Dennis pulled out his notebook. "Mind if I quote you on that?"

"Better keep me anonymous. I don't need trouble with the cops." Norm finally threw the frisbee back. "But I'll tell you this. It wasn't suicide."

"Did she swim alone?"

"No, she always swam with a swim buddy–Maureen or Stan from Circle Drive, or Mary Anne up on the bluff." Norm pointed toward the houses overlooking the cove. "Mary

Anne's got the place with the gazebo."

Dennis made notes. "Anyone else I should talk to?"

"Those are the ones who knew her best. But be careful how you approach them—Amelia's death has everyone pretty shaken up."

Dennis headed up to Circle Drive. The house Norm had indicated was a modest beachfront cottage with a clear view of Shaw's Cove. Dennis knocked, but no one answered. He was about to leave when he saw a woman pushing a stroller along the sidewalk.

"Excuse me," he called. "I'm looking for Maureen—do you know if she's home?"

The woman stopped and adjusted the stroller's blanket against the ocean breeze. Dennis recognized her from around town. "Sally, right? We've met before."

"Yes, but I'm sorry, I don't remember your name." She shielded her eyes from the sun with one hand.

"Dennis Driver. I'm with the Daily Pilot." He glanced down at the stroller and was surprised to see not a baby but a small, dignified-looking chihuahua. "That's quite a passenger you have there."

Sally's face brightened. "This is Jose. He's getting too old for long walks, but he still likes to get out and see the neighborhood." She gave the dog a gentle pat. "You're looking for Maureen?"

"Yes, I'm working on a story about Amelia Hart."

Sally's expression sobered. "Terrible thing. But Maureen and Stan are in Palm Springs for the week. They left right after they heard about Amelia."

"Any idea when they'll be back?"

"Not until next weekend, I think."

Dennis made a note. "What about Mary Anne? Do you know her?"

"Mary Anne Whitfield? Sure, but she's pretty shaken up about Amelia. They were close friends." Sally adjusted Jose's blanket again. "You might want to wait until after the funeral to talk to her."

"When's the funeral?"

"Friday morning at Saint Catherine's."

Dennis thanked Sally and drove up the hill to Mary Anne's house. It was an impressive property with high gates and a long driveway that disappeared behind eucalyptus trees.

He pressed the intercom button at the gate.

"Yes?" The voice was cautious, strained.

"Mrs. Whitfield? My name is Dennis Driver. I'm a reporter with the Daily Pilot, and I'm working on a story about Amelia Hart. I was hoping I could ask you a few questions."

There was a long pause, longer than simple grief would explain. "I'm sorry, but I really can't discuss her. Not yet."

"I understand. Would it be possible to speak with you after the funeral? I'd like to write something that honors her memory properly."

Another pause, and Dennis could hear what sounded like a television or radio in the background. "Perhaps. Call me next week."

The intercom went quiet, leaving Dennis with the sound of wind in the eucalyptus trees and the distant crash of waves below. Something in Mary Anne's tone suggested she was holding back more than just grief.

D ennis drove back into town with a list of names but little concrete information. Everyone seemed to agree that Amelia Hart wasn't the type to kill herself, but no one was ready to talk about what might have actually happened to her.

On impulse, he stopped at the William Fields Gallery on Coast Highway. Julie had mentioned that her mother was an artist as well as a collector. Maybe seeing Amelia's work would help him understand who she really was.

The gallery was sleek and intimidating, with white walls and expensive-looking pieces lit by carefully positioned spots.

A woman in a black dress looked up from her desk as he entered.

"Can I help you?"

"I'm Dennis Driver from the Daily Pilot. I'm writing about Amelia Hart, and I understand she was an artist. Do you have any of her paintings here?"

The woman's demeanor shifted, becoming more respectful. "Oh. I'm Fiona Miller. Yes, we represent Amelia's work." Her voice carried genuine sadness. "This is such a terrible loss for the art community."

Fiona led him toward the back of the gallery. "Amelia was incredibly talented. She worked in photorealism—paintings so detailed they looked like photographs. Very demanding technique."

She stopped in front of a large canvas that dominated the back wall. "This is one of her most powerful pieces. She painted it last year."

Dennis looked at the painting and felt his chest tighten. The subject was a battlefield scene: a wounded soldier being carried by a medic, both covered in mud and blood, the wounded man's face twisted in pain.

The painting blurred at the edges, replaced by memory. The gallery suddenly felt too warm. Dennis could hear his heartbeat in his ears, could smell jungle rot and smell the gun smoke. For a moment, he wasn't in Laguna Beach but back in Vietnam, crouched in elephant grass while artillery pounded the tree line.

"Are you all right?" Fiona's voice seemed to come from very far away.

The jungle faded. The gallery returned. Cold air on his neck. Fiona's voice reached him from across the void.

Dennis forced himself to breathe slowly, the way the Army

psychiatrist had taught him. Focus on the present. Gallery floor. Art lights. Ocean breeze through the open door.

"I'm fine," he said, though his voice sounded unsteady. "Her work is very... intense."

"Amelia said art should make people feel something, even if it's uncomfortable." Fiona studied his face with concern. "She believed in confronting difficult truths rather than looking away from them. Would you like some water?"

"No, thank you. I should go." Dennis headed for the door, needing air and space and distance from the painted battlefield.

Outside, he sat in his car for several minutes, waiting for his hands to stop shaking. The flashback had been brief but intense—a reminder that Vietnam wasn't as far behind him as he'd hoped.

But it also told him something crucial about Amelia Hart. A woman who painted wounded soldiers with such unflinching detail, who chose to confront rather than avoid life's harsh realities, didn't seem like someone who would give up and kill herself.

Dennis started his car and headed back to the office. He had a story to write, and for the first time since taking the assignment, he was beginning to understand the woman at the center of it.

Amelia Hart didn't look away from difficult truths. She painted them. The question was: had one of those truths gotten her killed?

6. WITHOUT AMELIA

The morning sun cast a hazy glow over the Los Angeles skyline as Wolf Schmidt's turquoise VW bus wheezed through traffic on the 405. The January air was warm—unusual for the season—and carried the familiar scent of exhaust and possibility.

"Hard to believe it's January," he said, navigating between lanes. "Must be seventy degrees."

Carol smoothed the peace sign sticker on the dashboard for the third time in ten minutes, her nervous energy betraying the casual conversation. "Do you think anyone will ask questions? About Amelia, I mean."

Wolf's grip on the steering wheel remained steady, his voice matter-of-fact. "Why would they? She had an accident. These things happen." He glanced at the tote bag on the floor between them, containing the Rix landscape. "We have our own concerns to manage now."

"It's just so sudden. One day she's planning her New Year's party, the next..." Carol's voice trailed off as she picked at her thumbnail—a habit that surfaced when she was working through problems. "Maybe we should slow down. Wait a few months before selling anything."

"Absolutely not." Wolf's response was immediate. "Sitting on inventory costs money. The studio rent, materials, our living expenses—they don't pause for grief."

Carol turned to face him fully. "She was talking about quitting, Wolf. The last few times I saw her, she kept saying the risks were getting too high."

"Amelia said many things when she'd been drinking," Wolf said, slowing to take the La Cienega exit.

"But what if she meant it this time? What if she was planning to—"

"She wasn't quitting. She was planning to open a gallery in Las Vegas." Wolf pulled into a parking space near Wilshire Boulevard.

He paused, studying the morning traffic. He didn't miss her. Not really. Just the way she thought three steps ahead of everyone else. Just the calm she brought when the margins got thin and buyers started asking too many questions.

A lpert Antiques and Gallery extended deep into the building, a maze of rooms filled with curated antiques. An elderly man looked up from his paperwork as they entered, squinting through thick glasses as if the modern world was slightly out of focus.

"Back again, are we?" Alpert said, though his tone suggested he wasn't entirely displeased. "What treasures have you brought me today, Mr...?"

"Fisher," Wolf replied smoothly. "Hans Fisher. I have something you might find interesting."

Wolf removed the painting from the tote bag with practiced

care. Alpert's expression shifted from mild interest to focused attention as he examined the Rix landscape, muttering under his breath about "real brushwork" and "none of this abstract nonsense."

"Julian Rix," Alpert announced, as if identifying a long-lost friend. "California school. Proper painting, not like the garbage they're calling art these days." He glared briefly toward a small Pollock reproduction on the far wall. "How did you acquire this?"

"Estate sale in Orange County," Wolf replied. "The family didn't appreciate what they had."

It was partly true. Amelia had found the original Rix signature on a damaged canvas at an estate sale six months ago. Wolf had spent three weeks recreating the painting from photographs and gallery catalogs, matching the brushwork and color palette perfectly. He had prepared the canvas, using techniques his father, an art restorer in Germany, had taught him for aging the canvas and priming it with period-appropriate ground.

Alpert examined the painting under a magnifying glass, checking the signature, the crack patterns in the paint, and the wear on the frame's corners. Wolf watched with calm confidence. He'd fooled Alpert before.

"Documentation?" Alpert asked, though his tone suggested he already expected the answer.

Wolf handed him a standard estate sale receipt. "Small estate. No provenance available."

Carol wandered the gallery's back rooms, her trained eye cataloging frames and canvases they might purchase. She'd developed a talent for spotting period frames that could be repurposed, often finding pieces that were more valuable than the paintings they held.

"It's good work," Alpert admitted, still studying the brush-strokes. "But you know how it is—California landscapes aren't moving like they used to. Too many people chasing the New York artists these days." He shook his head disapprovingly. "No appreciation for craftsmanship." "Fifteen hundred," Wolf said.

Alpert laughed, a sound like paper rustling. "Impossible. I'd be lucky to get twelve for it, and that's if I found the right collector."

Wolf began returning the painting to the tote bag. "Perhaps Sotheby's would be more appreciative."

"Wait, wait." Alpert's arthritic hand moved toward the painting. "Let me see it once more."

The negotiation continued for fifteen minutes, each man testing the other's resolve. Wolf had learned patience in these situations from Amelia—never seem desperate, never accept the first offer, always be prepared to walk away. She'd been brilliant at reading people, at knowing exactly when to push and when to retreat.

"Twelve hundred," Alpert finally offered, "and I'll include those frames your lady friend is admiring."

Wolf glanced at Carol, who had selected two ornate gilt frames perfect for their next projects. The frames were worth at least three hundred.

"Deal."

Alpert counted out twelve hundred-dollar bills with the satisfaction of a man who'd made a good purchase, then wrote a receipt in his careful script: *H. Fisher - $1200 - Rix landscape + 2 frames.*

· · ·

Walking back to the van, Wolf felt the satisfaction of a successful transaction. The money would keep their studio operational for another six weeks, maybe eight if they were careful with expenses.

"That went perfectly," Carol said, but her voice carried an undertone of worry. "Almost too perfectly. What if Alpert gets suspicious about Hans Fisher always having such good pieces?"

"Then Hans Fisher disappears and Heinrich Mueller takes his place," Wolf replied. "I have four complete identities prepared. Amelia insisted on redundancy."

Carol was quiet for several blocks, watching Los Angeles blur past the window. Finally, she said, "I keep thinking about what she said at Christmas. About having enough money to disappear somewhere warm."

Wolf started the van, his mind already calculating their next moves. "She also said we were sitting on a goldmine and only fools would abandon it."

"But what if someone else knew? About the forgeries, I mean." Carol's voice dropped to barely above a whisper. "What if that's why she—"

"Why, she what? Killed herself?" Wolf pulled into traffic, his tone remaining steady. "Amelia Hart didn't kill herself over business concerns, Carol. She was tougher than that."

He didn't add what he was really thinking: that Amelia had been more worried lately, more careful about checking locks and looking over her shoulder. She'd mentioned seeing the same car parked near her house twice in one week. But paranoia was an occupational hazard in their line of work.

"Where to next?" Carol asked, smoothing the peace sign sticker again.

"Art supply store for materials. Then the flea market." Wolf calculated their remaining inventory as he drove. "We have six pieces in various stages. Without Amelia's collector contacts, we'll need to rely more on small-time dealers like Alpert."

As they headed toward Hollywood, Wolf allowed himself one moment of uncertainty. Amelia had trained him for the technical work, for the careful process of creating paintings that could fool experts. What she hadn't trained him for was doing it alone, without her instinct for reading people and situations.

But he'd learn. He had to.

The alternative was admitting that Amelia Hart had been irreplaceable, and Wolf Schmidt had never been sentimental about business partnerships.

Even when they ended in Shaw's Cove after midnight.

7. BEAUTY AND GRIEF

Julie arrived at St. Catherine's Church forty minutes before her mother's funeral, partly because Aunt Carmen had insisted on punctuality, and partly because she couldn't stand waiting at home anymore.

The church felt different than her childhood Sunday services. Smaller somehow, and too quiet. Carmen was already there, of course, directing the funeral home staff with the same efficiency she brought to everything else. At fifty-eight, Carmen possessed a dignity that made others automatically defer to her—immaculate makeup, perfectly styled black hair, and a suit that fit like it had been designed specifically for this moment.

"The flowers are beautiful," Julie said, though she barely registered them.

Carmen embraced her gently, then took her hand. "Your mother would have been pleased. She always said funerals should have more beauty than sorrow."

They walked to the front pew together, Julie's black dress rustling against the polished wood. Around them, the church gradually filled with mourners—an eclectic mix of Amelia's friends from the art world. A man in a tie-dyed shirt and leather bell-bottoms sat next to a woman in a neon floral mini dress who kept her oversized sunglasses on despite being indoors.

Julie recognized some faces from her mother's parties: gallery owners, artists, collectors who'd bought Amelia's work. But there were others she didn't know. A couple near the back who seemed more interested in studying the other attendees than grieving. The man had silver-streaked hair and wore an expensive-looking jacket; the woman beside him kept checking her watch nervously.

Carmen's posture suddenly stiffened. Julie followed her gaze to see a tall, gray-haired man standing uncertainly near the entrance, Howie Bloom. He wore the kind of expensive suit that came with his new life as a movie producer.

"What's *he* doing here?" Carmen's voice could have frozen holy water.

"He's my father," Julie said quietly, standing up. "And he loved Mom too."

She walked back to meet him, aware of the murmurs from other mourners. Her father looked older than when she'd last seen him six months ago, but his eyes were clear—the kind of clarity that came with ten years of sobriety.

"Julie," he said, his voice carrying the careful cadence of someone who'd learned to weigh his words. "I wasn't sure... Carmen made it clear I wasn't welcome at family events."

"This isn't a family event, Dad. It's Mom's funeral." Julie took his arm. "She would have wanted you here."

Carmen's disapproval radiated from the front pew as Julie led Howie to sit beside her. The silence between the three of them was heavy with decades of history—his drinking, the divorce, the years of missed birthdays and holidays.

"How are you holding up?" he asked quietly.

"I don't know yet," Julie admitted. "It doesn't feel real. Like I'm watching someone else's life from the back row."

The church filled steadily. Julie noticed Detective Stone slip in near the back, probably hoping to observe the mourners for suspicious behavior. Near him sat a young man with a notebook—the reporter from the Daily Pilot who'd interviewed her.

The silver-haired man from earlier caught her attention again when he gave a subtle nod to someone across the aisle. Julie followed his gaze but couldn't tell who had acknowledged him. Something about the exchange felt deliberate, calculated.

A soft sound at the entrance drew everyone's attention. The casket appeared, carried by six men in dark suits, preceded by Father Martinez swinging a silver censer. The incense filled the air with its familiar scent, bringing back memories of Sunday mornings when everything felt safe and permanent.

As the casket moved down the aisle, Julie felt her composure begin to crack. Howie's hand found hers, steady and warm. Even Carmen reached over to squeeze her other hand.

Father Martinez began the service with traditional prayers, but Julie barely heard them. She was thinking about the last conversation she'd had with her mother, about the concert she'd chosen over staying home for New Year's Eve, about all the things she'd never get to say now.

"Carmen Montez will now speak about her sister, Amelia," Father Martinez announced.

Carmen approached the podium with characteristic poise, though Julie could see the slight tremor in her hands.

"We're here to remember my sister Amelia—Amy to those who knew her best," Carmen began, her voice steady. "Amy was an artist in every sense of the word. She saw beauty where others saw ordinary things, and she had the gift of showing that beauty to the rest of us."

Julie watched her aunt's face, seeing the genuine love beneath her composed exterior.

"She was also a devoted mother who raised Julie to be strong and independent. Amy believed in living fully, whether she was painting in her studio or swimming in the ocean she loved." Carmen's voice caught slightly. "She taught us that life is short, but art endures. Her paintings will continue to bring joy long after we're gone."

Carmen paused, looking directly at Julie. "Amy wouldn't want us to dwell in sadness. She'd want us to celebrate the time we had with her and to keep creating, keep living, keep finding beauty in the world."

As Carmen returned to her seat, Father Martinez called Julie to speak. She hadn't wanted to do this. Not really. What could you say that didn't sound like a thank-you card taped to a tombstone? But she walked to the podium anyway, her prepared remarks suddenly feeling inadequate.

"My mother was many things," Julie began, gripping the sides of the podium. "She was an artist, a collector, a woman who threw legendary parties. But to me, she was just Mom— the person who made pancakes shaped like flowers on Sunday mornings and who taught me that it was okay to be different."

She looked out at the sea of faces, some familiar, some strange. The nervous woman near the back checked her watch again, as if she had somewhere more important to be.

"Mom had a way of making everyone feel special. She'd remember your favorite color, or the name of your dog, or that story you told her six months ago. She made people feel seen."

Julie's voice grew stronger as she found her rhythm. "She

wasn't perfect. She worried too much, and she had very strong opinions about everything from art to politics to how to load a dishwasher properly. But she loved fiercely, and she lived completely."

She paused, looking at the casket. "I'm going to miss her terrible jokes and her good advice. I'm going to miss the way she'd get so excited about a new painting that she'd wake me at six in the morning to describe it. Most of all, I'm going to miss having her in my corner, believing I could do anything."

Julie stepped down from the podium and touched the casket briefly, her fingertips lingering on the polished wood. "I love you, Mom."

The service concluded with more prayers and a hymn that echoed off the stone walls. Julie noticed the silver-haired couple slip out just before the final verse ended.

As the pallbearers prepared to carry the casket out, Howie leaned close to her ear.

"Some of these people," he said quietly, "they don't look like they're here to grieve. They look like they're here to make sure she's really dead."

Julie followed his gaze to where the couple had been sitting, now seeing only space. Something was calculating about how they'd observed everyone, something that made her suddenly uncomfortable.

"Did you see them leave?" she whispered.

Howie nodded. "Right before the last song. Like they'd gotten what they came for."

As they filed out of the church behind the casket, Julie found herself scanning the faces around her with new aware- ness. The procession to the cemetery would be small—just family and close friends. But Julie couldn't shake the feeling that among the genuine mourners, someone had attended not to honor her mother's memory, but to satisfy themselves that Amelia Hart was truly gone.

And that someone might be the person who'd killed her.

The January air felt sharp against her face as they emerged from the church, but the chill running down her spine had nothing to do with the weather. Somewhere in that crowd of mourners, her mother's killer might have just said goodbye.

8. THE DEALER

Ray Stone stepped into the William Fields Gallery and immediately felt out of place. The white walls and polished floors reflected a world where aesthetics mattered more than truth, where everything was carefully arranged to create an impression rather than reveal reality.

The gallery occupied a prime spot on Coast Highway, its large windows displaying paintings that probably cost more than most people's cars. Ray had driven past it dozens of times since moving to Laguna Beach, but he'd never imagined he'd be here investigating a murder.

William Fields emerged from his office with the smile of someone accustomed to managing wealthy clients. He was impeccably dressed in a charcoal suit that probably cost more than Ray's monthly salary, but there was something strained about his composure. Ray noticed how Fields immediately began aligning the already-perfect row of pens on his desk— once, twice, then abandoning the task when he caught himself.

"Detective Stone, I assume this is about Amelia's tragic accident." Fields' voice carried just the right note of sorrow, but his eyes were calculating, measuring how much he needed to reveal.

"Actually, we're treating Mrs. Hart's death as suspicious," Ray said, watching Fields' reaction carefully. "I understand you represented her work?"

Fields gestured toward a section of the gallery where several paintings hung under carefully positioned lights, his eyes lingering on one particular piece—a small landscape that seemed oddly placed among Amelia's photorealistic works. "Amelia was one of our most promising artists. Her style was just starting to command real attention." He paused, his expression darkening. "Her death is a tremendous loss for the art community."

Ray approached the paintings, studying the meticulous detail that made them look like photographs. "How long had you been working together?"

"About three years. I gave her first solo show here in 1967." Fields followed Ray, but his gaze kept drifting back to that small landscape. "She was incredibly talented, but the market for contemporary realism takes time to develop."

"Was she making a living from her art?"

Fields hesitated, and Ray caught the pause. "The art business is... unpredictable. Some months are better than others."

Ray decided to push. "I've heard rumors that Amelia had some financial troubles. Debts, maybe?"

Fields went still, his hand frozen halfway to his tie. "Where did you hear that?"

"It's a small town, Mr. Fields. People talk." Ray kept his voice neutral. "Is it true?"

Fields walked to his desk and sat down, his fingers once again reaching for the pens before he stopped himself. "She...

made some poor decisions. Vegas, mostly." The words came reluctantly, as if pulled from him against his will.

Ray felt his attention sharpen. The way Fields said "Amelia" was too polished, too rehearsed. It felt off., like a name he'd practiced mourning. "What kind of poor decisions?"

"Gambling," Fields said quietly. "She'd been going to Las Vegas regularly. She told me she'd had some bad luck recently."

"How do you know about her gambling, Mr. Fields?"

"She confided in me." Fields' voice was carefully modulated. "Amelia was more than just a client. We'd become friends over the years. She trusted me with her concerns."

Ray made notes, watching as Fields glanced again at the small landscape painting. "What specifically did she tell you?"

Fields leaned back in his chair, choosing his words carefully. "She said she'd gotten in over her head. Made some bets she couldn't cover. She was worried about the consequences."

"Did she say how much money she owed?"

"No specific amounts. But from her anxiety level, I gathered it was substantial." Fields paused, then added, "She asked me about advancing her money against future sales."

"Did you give her an advance?"

"I considered it. But we operate on margins thinner than our frames, and..." Fields started to reach for his pens again, caught himself, and clasped his hands together. "I wasn't sure it was wise to enable her gambling problem."

Ray studied Fields' face. The man seemed genuinely conflicted, but something about his detailed knowledge of Amelia's troubles bothered Ray. "When did she first tell you about the gambling?"

"A few months ago. She seemed embarrassed about it, but

she needed someone to..." Fields stopped abruptly, as if he'd been about to say too much.

"Someone to what?"

"Someone to talk to," Fields finished, but Ray sensed that wasn't what he'd originally intended to say.

"Was anyone else aware of her gambling?"

"I don't think so. Amelia was private about personal matters." Fields stood and walked to the window overlooking Coast Highway. "That's why her death is so shocking. She seemed to be managing everything so well."

Ray sensed an opening. "But she wasn't managing well, was she? If she needed money badly enough to ask for advances?"

The color drained from Fields' face like someone had dimmed a light. "The gambling made everything worse. But her art sales hadn't been strong lately either. I attended her New Year's Eve party," Fields added, as if trying to change the subject. "She seemed in good spirits that night. I had no idea she was contemplating..." He didn't finish the sentence.

"What time did you leave the party?"

"Around twelve-thirty. My wife gets tired at late events."

"Did Amelia seem intoxicated when you left?"

Fields considered the question. "She'd been drinking, but she was perfectly coherent. Amelia had a high tolerance for alcohol."

Ray looked around the gallery, taking in the expensive fixtures and prime real estate. "Business must be good to afford a location like this."

"We do well enough," Fields said carefully. "Though the overhead is substantial."

"Would Amelia's death affect your business significantly?"

Fields stiffened at the question. "I'm not sure what you're implying, Detective."

"I'm not implying anything. I'm asking if losing a major artist would create financial problems for you."

"Amelia was important to us, but we represent many artists." Fields' voice had grown defensive. "Besides, her death will likely increase the value of her existing work. That's unfortunately how the art market works."

Ray noted the contradiction—Fields claiming Amelia wasn't crucial to his business while acknowledging that her death would boost the value of her paintings. Someone stood to profit from Amelia Hart's death, and William Fields was in a position to benefit significantly.

"I'll need a list of everyone who attended the party," Ray said, closing his notebook.

"Of course. I'll have my assistant prepare that for you."

As Ray walked toward the door, he turned back. "One more question, Mr. Fields. If Amelia was as desperate for money as you suggest, might she have done something... irregular to get it?"

Fields went completely still. "What do you mean?"

"I mean, someone with gambling debts and declining sales might be tempted to take shortcuts. Forge signatures, misrepresent authenticity, that sort of thing."

"Amelia would never..." Fields began, then stopped himself, his eyes darting once more to that small landscape painting. "She was completely honest in her business dealings."

But Ray caught the hesitation, the moment when Fields almost said something else. The gallery owner knew more about Amelia's financial situation than he was admitting, and possibly more about how she'd been trying to solve her problems.

Ray left the gallery with more questions than answers—but one certainty: William Fields was hiding something. And in a business where deception could be lucrative, that made him dangerous.

As he walked to his car, Ray found himself thinking about that small landscape painting Fields kept glancing at, and wondering what secrets were hidden behind the polished facade of Laguna Beach's art world, whether one of those secrets had been worth killing for remained to be seen.

9. WOUNDS AND CLUES

Dennis sat in Dr. Harris's office, trying to explain why a painting in an art gallery had sent him into a panic attack three days earlier.

The office occupied the converted study of Dr. Harris's South Laguna home, its warm lighting and book-lined walls designed to put patients at ease. Dr. Harris himself was a man in his fifties who navigated his wheelchair with practiced efficiency, his sharp eyes reflecting the intelligence that had made him one of Orange County's most respected psychiatrists.

"Tell me about this investigation," Dr. Harris said, setting down his pen. "What draws you to the Amelia Hart case?"

Dennis shifted in his chair, still uncomfortable discussing his work. "Everyone's saying she killed herself, but something doesn't add up. The way people act when I ask questions—they're hiding something."

"And how do you know they're hiding something?"

"Same way I knew when villagers were lying about VC activity." Dennis paused, realizing what he'd said. "Body language, inconsistencies, the way they won't meet your eyes. In Vietnam, reading people wrong could get you killed."

Dr. Harris made a note. "So your military experience helps with journalism?"

"Sometimes." Dennis rubbed his arm unconsciously. "But other times, like with that painting, it works against me. The war scene was so realistic that suddenly I was back in Hue during Tet. I could smell the gunpowder, the decay. The sweat trickling down my spine, the grip of my M-16 digging into my palm. I hadn't held that rifle in years—but my hands remembered."

"Describe what happened physically."

Dennis's hand moved to his chest. "Heart racing, couldn't breathe, felt like someone was sitting on my chest. I had to get out of there."

"That's a panic attack," Dr. Harris confirmed. "Are you having trouble sleeping?"

"Yeah. And when I do sleep, I dream about the firefight. But lately, the dreams are mixed up with this investigation. I see Amelia Hart floating in Shaw's Cove, but she's wearing jungle fatigues." Dennis looked embarrassed. "Sounds crazy, I know."

"Not crazy at all. Your mind is processing two types of violence—what you experienced in Vietnam and what you're investigating now." Dr. Harris leaned forward. "Tell me about the people you've interviewed. What makes you think they're lying?"

Dennis considered the question. "There's this gallery owner, William Fields. When he talks about Amelia's financial problems, he gets nervous—fidgets with things on his desk, won't maintain eye contact. In Vietnam, we learned that liars have tells. Fields has them in spades."

"What about the family?"

"Amelia's daughter Julie seems genuine. Her grief is real. But there's something she's not telling me—maybe something she doesn't even realize she knows." Dennis paused. "And there was this couple at the funeral. They watched everyone else instead of participating in the service. They left early, like they'd gotten what they came for."

"Your observation skills from military intelligence are serving you well," Dr. Harris noted. "But they're also triggering your trauma responses. How are you managing that?"

Dennis looked uncomfortable. "I smoke marijuana sometimes. It helps with the anxiety."

"And does it affect your work?"

"Not really. If anything, it helps me think more clearly about the case. Less worried about my own reactions, more focused on what people are telling me." Dennis met Dr. Harris's eyes. "Is that wrong?"

"For now, if it's helping you function, I won't recommend stopping. But I'd like to prescribe some medication that might help with both the anxiety and the nightmares." Dr. Harris wrote on his prescription pad. "Imipramine should help with the depression and anxiety. It's relatively new but showing good results. Seconal will help with sleep, but it's strong. Use it only at night, and tell me if you feel groggy or disconnected during the day."

Dennis took the prescription, studying the unfamiliar drug names. "Will these change how I think? I need to stay sharp for this story."

"They should actually help you think more clearly by reducing the background anxiety. Your military training gave you valuable skills—the ability to read people, to notice details others miss, to stay calm under pressure. The medication will help you access those skills without being overwhelmed by trauma responses."

"There's something else," Dennis said hesitantly. "I keep

thinking about the Amelia Hart painting that triggered my attack. It showed a wounded soldier being carried by a medic. What if that's connected to her death somehow?"

"How do you mean?"

Dennis leaned forward, his voice growing more intense. "She chose to paint that scene. She bought similar paintings. She could have painted sunsets, or still lifes, or ocean views. But she chose blood and anguish. Why?" He paused, working through the thought. "Not because she liked it. Because she recognized it. And maybe... because she needed someone else to recognize it, too."

Dr. Harris made another note. "That's a perceptive observation. Your trauma may actually be making you more sensitive to the psychological states of others."

"You think so?"

"People who've experienced violence can often recognize it in others—even when it's hidden. Your panic attack at the gallery might have been triggered not just by the war imagery, but by some unconscious recognition that the artist herself had experienced trauma."

Dennis felt something click into place. "She was afraid of something. Her daughter said she wouldn't swim in the ocean at night, but that's where they found her body."

"What does your instinct tell you about that?"

"That someone forced her into a situation she feared. And whoever did it knew her well enough to understand her vulnerabilities." Dennis looked up at Dr. Harris. "What if the paintings were her way of saying she was in danger? What if she was documenting her own trauma, hoping someone would understand?"

"It sounds like the analysis of someone trained to gather

intelligence and assess threats. The key is learning to trust your instincts without letting them overwhelm you."

As Dennis prepared to leave, Dr. Harris offered one final observation. "Your war experience was traumatic, but it also gave you skills that make you an exceptional investigator. The challenge is learning to use those skills without being consumed by them."

Walking to his car, Dennis felt something he hadn't experienced in months: hope not just for his own recovery, but for finding the truth about Amelia Hart. His trauma wasn't just a burden—it was also a tool, a way of understanding violence and deception that others might miss.

Amelia Hart had painted scenes of suffering and fear because she'd recognized those emotions in her own life. She'd surrounded herself with images of trauma because she was living it. And if Dennis was right, those paintings weren't just art—they were a cry for help that no one had heard in time.

The prescription crinkled in his pocket as he drove back toward Laguna Beach. Still, for the first time since returning from Vietnam, the promise of medication felt less like surrender and more like preparation for the investigation ahead.

He had work to do, and for the first time, he felt equipped to do it.

10. NOTHING TO HIDE

Ray Stone studied Wolfgang Schmidt across the interview table at the Laguna Beach Police Department. The man sat with the composed stillness of someone who'd learned to control his reactions under scrutiny.

Wolf wore paint-stained jeans and a work shirt, but there was nothing casual about his attention. His eyes moved with the same precision Ray had seen in crime scene photographers, cataloging details, measuring distances. Even in the sterile interview room, he carried himself with the quiet confidence of someone who knew exactly how much to reveal.

"Thank you for coming in, Mr. Schmidt," Ray began, settling into his chair. "I understand you knew Amelia Hart well."

"We shared a studio," Wolf replied, his accent lending a slight formality to the words. "We were colleagues."

Ray made a note. "How long had you been working together?"

"Two years, approximately. Amelia had established connections in the local art community. She helped me find my place here."

"What kind of work did you do together?"

Wolf's pause was so brief that Ray almost missed it. "We painted. Sometimes we discussed technique or the business aspects of selling art. Amelia understood the market better than most."

"Tell me about New Year's Eve. You attended her party?"

"Yes. My wife Carol was feeling unwell, so I went alone." Wolf's hands remained folded on the table, completely still. "Amelia threw excellent parties. Good wine, interesting conversation."

Ray leaned forward slightly. "What time did you arrive?"

"Around nine-thirty. The party was already well underway."

"And what time did you leave?"

"Close to two in the morning. I was among the last guests to depart."

Ray felt his attention sharpen. While Wolf's expression didn't change, Ray caught a slight tightening around his eyes.

"I stayed to help Amelia lock up."

"So it was just you and Amelia for the final hour?"

"Yes. We were discussing business matters." Wolf met Ray's eyes steadily. "She seemed in good spirits, though.

Perhaps she'd had more wine than usual."

"What kind of business matters?"

Wolf considered his answer carefully. "Gallery representation, upcoming shows. The practical concerns of working artists." He paused. "Amelia was exploring new opportunities."

"Such as?"

"She mentioned interest from collectors in Las Vegas. The gambling crowd likes to put their winnings in art and other tangibles." Wolf's expression remained neutral. "She was considering expanding her market there."

Ray made another note, thinking about what William Fields had told him about Amelia's gambling problems. "Did she seem worried about anything? Financial pressures, personal problems?"

"Amelia was always concerned about money. Art is an unpredictable profession." Wolf shifted slightly in his chair. "But she was optimistic about her prospects."

"Mr. Schmidt, I've heard that Amelia had gambling debts. Did she ever discuss that with you?"

For just a fraction of a second, Wolf's composed mask slipped. Ray caught a flicker of something. Surprise? Recognition? Fear? Then the neutral expression returned, smooth as paint over a crack.

"She mentioned visiting Las Vegas occasionally. I assumed it was for meeting collectors."

"You never got the impression she was in financial trouble?"

"Amelia lived well. Beautiful house, expensive art collection. If she had serious debts, she hid them effectively."

Ray studied Wolf's face, looking for more tells. The man was remarkably controlled, but that momentary crack when gambling was mentioned hadn't gone unnoticed.

"After you left the party, where did you go?"

"Home to my wife. She was sleeping, so I tried not to wake her."

"Anyone else who can verify your whereabouts after two AM?"

Wolf's slight smile held no warmth. "I'm afraid not. Carol takes medication for sleep. She rarely wakes during the night."

Ray made another note. No alibi for the critical hours when

Amelia had died. "Tell me about your studio arrangement. Where is it located?"

"A warehouse space in Laguna Canyon. We split the rent and shared some equipment—easels, lighting, storage for canvases." Wolf's voice remained even, but he seemed to be choosing his words more carefully now. "It's quite spacious, actually. Two separate work areas, plus a common space for larger pieces. We also maintain a small office area for business correspondence and a storage room for supplies and finished works."

Ray noticed the over-explanation. Most people answered direct questions directly. Wolf was painting a picture—literally and figuratively.

"Did you store any of Amelia's work there?"

"Some pieces, yes. Works in progress, or paintings she hadn't yet decided how to market."

"I'll need to take a look at the studio."

"Of course. However, I should mention that I've been reorganizing since Amelia's death. Sorting through which materials belonged to whom."

Ray felt a flicker of suspicion. "When did you start this reorganization?"

"Yesterday. It seemed appropriate to settle our business arrangements now that she's gone."

"Very efficient of you."

Wolf met his gaze without flinching. "Grief is a luxury I cannot afford. I have rent to pay and commissions to complete."

The cold practicality of the statement struck Ray as either refreshingly honest or calculated callousness. "Did Amelia seem different lately? Anxious, scared, excited about something?"

"She was focused on expanding her business. Perhaps more driven than usual." Wolf paused, as if debating whether to continue. "She had been working longer hours, staying at the studio later into the evening."

"Working on what?"

"A new series. Very detailed pieces. She was experimenting with techniques to make her paintings even more photorealistic." Wolf's fingers drummed once against the table, the first nervous gesture Ray had observed. "Demanding work. She was a perfectionist about it."

"Can you think of anyone who might have wanted to harm Amelia?"

Wolf was quiet for a long moment, his eyes focused somewhere beyond Ray's shoulder. "Amelia was successful, which always creates envy. But harm her?" He shook his head. "She was careful about the people she trusted."

"Careful how?"

"She didn't reveal personal information easily. Even after two years of working together, there was much about her life I didn't know." Wolf's expression remained neutral. "Perhaps that carefulness wasn't enough."

Ray closed his notebook and stood. "I appreciate your time, Mr. Schmidt. I may have more questions as the investigation continues."

Wolf rose as well, extending his hand. "Of course. I want whoever did this to be caught."

As they shook hands, Ray noticed the strength in Wolf's grip, the calluses that spoke of years working with his hands. Strong enough to overpower someone, skilled enough to make it look like an accident.

"One more thing," Ray said as Wolf reached the door. "The shared studio—do you plan to keep it?"

"I'm not sure yet. It holds too many memories of Amelia." Wolf's voice softened slightly, the first genuine emotion Ray had detected. "Perhaps it's time for a fresh start."

After Wolf left, Ray sat alone in the interview room, reviewing his notes. Wolfgang Schmidt was intelligent, controlled, and nearly impossible to read. He'd answered every question without quite giving away anything useful. His story was mostly consistent, but that reaction to the gambling question suggested he knew more than he was saying.

Most troubling was his immediate move to reorganize the studio. Either Wolf was genuinely settling business affairs, or he was destroying evidence. The discrepancy about when he left the party was also worth noting. Why would he stay so much later than other guests?

Wolf Schmidt remained at the top of his suspect list, but Ray was beginning to understand why the man might be difficult to catch. He had the patience of an artist—and the instincts of a man who knew how to make things disappear.

The question was: what exactly was Wolf Schmidt hiding, and how many secrets had he already erased?

11. THE HEIR APPARENT

Dennis parked outside the downtown LA law offices where Carmen Montez worked. Amelia's sister had agreed to meet with him after his call yesterday, and he hoped she might provide insights the police had missed. Getting family members to talk was always delicate. Grief made people either clam up completely or spill everything at once.

Carmen's corner office reflected her success as a probate attorney—expensive furniture, framed degrees, a view of the city skyline. But her eyes carried the weight of recent loss, and Dennis noticed how she kept a framed photo of two women at a beach positioned where she could see it while working.

"Thank you for seeing me," Dennis said, setting up his recorder after getting her permission. "I know this is difficult, but I'm trying to understand who your sister really was. Sometimes, family sees things differently than the outside world."

Carmen nodded, her lawyer's composure intact but not impenetrable. "Amelia was complicated. Brilliant, but she made choices that worried me." She paused, seeming to weigh her words. "I handled her late husband's estate. James Hart.

That's how I know there were... financial pressures she didn't talk about publicly."

"What kind of pressures?"

"Gambling debts. She was good at hiding it, but I saw the signs—borrowing against the house, selling jewelry, asking about liquidating assets from James's trust."

Dennis made notes, feeling pieces click into place. "Was she getting help? Treatment?"

"She claimed she was, but..." Carmen shrugged. "Amelia was proud. She wouldn't admit how bad things had gotten, even to family."

"What about Julie? Did she know?"

"Some of it. Enough to be worried sick." Carmen's expression hardened slightly. "That girl has been through enough, losing her father and now this. She doesn't deserve to lose everything because of Amelia's addiction."

Dennis caught the protective edge in her voice. "Everything?"

Carmen was quiet for a moment, and Dennis recognized the look of a lawyer deciding how much to reveal. "There's something else you should know," she said finally. "James Hart's trust splits the estate between Amelia and his son, Jack. The house alone is worth nearly three million dollars."

Dennis looked up sharply from his notes. "Jack? James Hart had another child?"

"From his first marriage. Jack Hart, about fifty now. Lives in Newport Beach, I think." Carmen's tone stayed professionally neutral, but Dennis sensed something underneath. "With Amelia dead, he inherits half of the remaining estate."

Carmen's voice cracked slightly before she caught herself, her hand unconsciously moving to grip the framed photo of the sisters. "If someone killed Amelia for money, Jack would be the prime suspect, at least in my mind."

"Tell me about Jack. What's he like?"

Carmen hesitated. "I don't know him well—I only met him a few times during the estate proceedings after James died. He seemed... polite in the way some people are when they've already decided what they want from you. Like he was calculating."

"Has he been in contact since Amelia's death?"

"He called the day after. Asked questions about the estate timeline. Jack Hart stands to inherit half the net value of the Laguna house, over a million dollars." Carmen's voice carried steel now, even as her fingers remained wrapped around the photo frame.

Dennis understood. Carmen wasn't just sharing information—she was directing him toward Jack to protect Julie's interests. Smart move for a probate attorney, and it aligned with his investigative instincts.

"I'll need to talk to him. Do you have his contact information?"

Carmen already had a business card ready, too ready, Dennis thought. "His office is in Newport Beach."

Dennis pocketed the card. "When did Jack first learn about the inheritance structure? Was it recent, or has he known since his father died?"

"He knew about the trust terms, what he stood to inherit, since his father set it up. "

"And he knew about Amelia's gambling?"

Carmen paused. "I don't know for certain. But if he was paying attention..." She gestured toward a stack of legal documents. "There were signs. The borrowing, the asset questions.

Anyone looking closely at the estate finances might have noticed."

Dennis felt the investigation shifting focus. A stepson with a million-dollar motive who knew about Amelia's vulnerabilities. Someone with legitimate access to information about her situation. Someone the family didn't know well enough to suspect immediately.

"What's your gut feeling about Jack?" he asked.

Carmen met his eyes directly. "My gut feeling is that my sister is dead, my niece might lose her home, and Jack Hart is about to become very wealthy. As an attorney, I'd say that deserves a closer look."

Dennis gathered his notes, mind already working through next steps. Jack Hart's contact information, his whereabouts on New Year's Eve, his financial situation, and his exact relationship with Amelia—all concrete leads to pursue.

"Thank you for this," he said, standing. "I know it wasn't easy."

"Find the truth," Carmen said. "Julie deserves that much."

Walking to his car, Dennis felt the satisfaction of a real breakthrough. Jack Hart was a suspect with a clear motive. Whether Carmen was manipulating him toward Jack to protect Julie or genuinely suspected her step-nephew didn't matter. The lead was solid either way.

Time to take a drive to Newport Beach.

12. THIRTY DAYS

Julie heard Jack's car in the driveway and took a steadying breath. His message had been brief and cold. He wanted to discuss "listing the house." As if it were just another piece of real estate, not the only home she'd ever known.

When she opened the door, Jack pushed past her without waiting for an invitation. She hadn't seen him for three years. He looked older than she remembered; overweight, thinning hair going gray, pale skin that suggested too much time indoors..

"Jack." She kept her voice neutral.

He was already surveying the living room with calculating eyes, straightening a crooked painting as he passed. "The place looks the same. Amelia never was one for change." His tone made it sound like a criticism, and the casual way he adjusted Mom's artwork, as if he had the right, made Julie's jaw clench.

"What did you want to discuss?"

Jack settled into her mother's old chair without asking, making himself at home. But his gaze drifted to the large landscape painting above the mantle, one of Mom's favorites, and lingered there a beat too long before he answered.

"The market's good right now. We should list while prices are high. I've talked to a realtor. She thinks we can get three-point-two, maybe three-point-five million."

We. As if he'd contributed anything to this house. "I want to buy out your half," Julie said before he could continue.

Jack's eyebrow rose, and she caught something that might have been amusement. "With what money?"

Heat flushed her cheeks. "I can raise one and a half million. Mom's art collection has to be worth that much."

"Even if it is, that could take a while," Jack said, leaning back in the chair. "Look, I'm not trying to be cruel here. But I've got creditors breathing down my neck. The oil business is hemorrhaging money, and I can't afford to let assets sit around gathering dust."

"What happened to your business?" The question slipped out before she could stop it.

His jaw tightened. "The old wells aren't producing enough to cover expenses." He brushed imaginary dust from the side table, dismissive. "The point is, I need liquidity now, not someday."

"Okay, okay. I'll have the collection appraised as soon as possible. Some of those pieces might be worth a lot of money."

Jack laughed, gesturing toward the walls with obvious disdain. "Art collection? You mean those paintings she bought at weekend galleries? Julie, that's not a collection, that's decoration."

"You don't know what you're talking about." But doubt crept into her voice. What if he was right? What if Mom's paintings were just pretty pictures worth a few thousand dollars each?

Jack must have heard the uncertainty because his expression softened into something that might have been pity. "Look, even if some of them are worth something, you're talking about maybe fifty, sixty thousand total. That's not even close to what you need."

"I don't know that yet. Neither do you."

"Fine." He shrugged, but his eyes flicked back to the landscape painting. "Get your appraisal. But I'm not waiting around indefinitely while you chase fantasies. You've got thirty days to come up with an offer for my half—one and a half million, cash. If you can't do it, we list the house."

"Thirty days?" Her stomach dropped. "That's not enough time to—"

"It's plenty of time to get art appraised and figure out if you're living in reality or not." Jack stood, smoothing his shirt over his paunch. "I'll arrange for an official property appraisal too, so that we're all working with real numbers."

Julie followed him to the door, her mind racing. Thirty days. How was she supposed to raise one and a half million dollars in thirty days?

"Jack, wait." He turned back, and for a moment she almost asked him to reconsider, to give her more time. But the expression on his face—patient, patronizing, already certain of the outcome—stopped her cold.

"What?"

"Nothing. I'll have an answer for you in thirty days."

After he left, Julie poured herself a glass of wine and sank onto the couch. The house felt different now, as if Jack's presence had contaminated it somehow. Everything looked the same, but now she saw it through Jack's eyes—square footage, resale value, renovation potential as if memories could be priced per square foot.

She took a sip of wine and tried to think practically. The art collection was her only real asset. Mom had been buying pieces for twenty years, always claiming she had "a good eye" for emerging artists. But what if Jack was right? What if they were just expensive decorations?

No. She couldn't think like that. Not yet.

Tomorrow she'd start making calls to appraisers, art dealers, anyone who might help her understand what she was really working with. And if the paintings weren't worth enough... well, she'd figure out another way. She had to.

The alternative was watching strangers walk through her home, packing up twenty-five years of memories, handing the keys to someone who would probably change it beyond recognition—was unthinkable.

Julie took another sip of wine and started making a mental list. Thirty days wasn't much time, but it was what she had. She'd make it work.

She had to.

13. GATED AND GUARDED

R ay started working through Amelia's guest list at Emerald Bay, an upscale gated community where four of the party guests lived. The security guard checked his badge and resident list before waving him through with directions to the Porter and Gibbs homes.

He drove past manicured lawns, luxury cars, and tennis courts visible through the palms. Ray had worked enough cases in places like this to know that money didn't prevent murder, just made it more complicated.

Mrs. Porter answered her door in tennis whites. "Is there something suspicious about Amelia's death?" she asked, and Ray caught the hint of excitement underneath her concern.

"Just following up on some details," Ray said. "I understand you were at her New Year's Eve party?"

"Yes, terrible thing. Such a shock." Mrs. Porter invited him in, gesturing toward an immaculate living room. "Though I have to say, there have been rumors."

"What kind of rumors?"

"Well, people are saying she might have killed herself.

Financial troubles, you know." Mrs. Porter leaned forward conspiratorially. "I didn't want to speak ill of the dead, but Amelia did seem off lately. Just last week, she stormed out of a doubles match in the middle of a set. Said something about having 'more important things to deal with.'

Very unlike her."

"Did she say what those things were?"

"No, but Carol Mitchell saw her arguing with some man in a dark car outside the grocery store a few days later. Carol said Amelia looked upset, not angry upset, but scared upset."

Ray made notes. Interesting, but could be anything. "Did you notice anything unusual at the party? Anyone who seemed out of place?"

Mrs. Porter shook her head. "No, I knew most everyone there. It was the usual crowd of neighbors and some of Amelia's art friends."

After twenty minutes of similar responses, Ray thanked Mrs. Porter and drove down the hill to Leonard Gibbs' house. The famous novelist answered the door looking like he'd been wrestling with a difficult chapter—unshaven, rumpled t-shirt, coffee-stained shorts.

"Detective Stone? Come in, come in. I was just thinking about poor Amelia." Gibbs led him into a marble-floored foyer lined with bookshelves. "Terrible business. How can I help?"

Ray appreciated the direct approach. "Tell me about the party. Did you notice anything unusual? Anyone who seemed out of place?"

Gibbs nodded immediately. "Actually, yes. There was a guy there I didn't recognize. Vinny something. Vincent, maybe? Didn't get his last name."

Ray's attention sharpened. This was the first concrete lead he'd gotten. "Tell me about Vinny. What did he look like?"

"Mid-forties, I'd guess. Silver-streaked hair, well-dressed, gold watch, that kind of thing. But there was something about him..." Gibbs paused, choosing his words. "He had that polished tough-guy vibe. You know the type— charming smile but hard eyes."

"How did he interact with Amelia?"

"That's what was interesting. They clearly knew each other well. I saw them talking privately by the pool area for maybe twenty minutes. Looked like a serious conversation."

Ray leaned forward. "Serious how? Friendly? Argumentative?"

"Hard to say from a distance, but their body language seemed... intense. Not hostile exactly, but not casual chitchat either."

"When did he arrive? When did he leave?"

Gibbs thought for a moment. "He came maybe an hour after the party started, around ten-thirty, and left before midnight. I remember because most of us stayed to watch the ball drop, but he was gone by then."

Ray made detailed notes. This was the kind of specific information he needed. "Did anyone else interact with him? Did he seem to know other guests?"

"He mostly kept to himself or stayed near Amelia. Polite enough when introduced, but didn't really mingle."

"Anything else you remember about him? The car he drove? How did he seem when he left?"

"BMW, I think. Dark blue or black. And when he left..." Gibbs frowned. "This might sound like a writer's imagination, but he seemed agitated. Not angry exactly, but wound up about something."

Ray finished his notes and handed Gibbs his card. "This is helpful. If you remember anything else about Vinny or that night, call me immediately."

"Of course." Gibbs walked him to the door. "Detective, do you think Amelia's death wasn't suicide?"

Ray hesitated. He couldn't share details, but Gibbs had been helpful. "Let's just say we're being thorough."

Driving back to the station, Ray's mind worked through the new information. Earlier that morning, the ME had called with a significant detail that somehow got left out of the original autopsy report.. The victim had chlorine in her lungs. Not ocean water. Pool water.

The chlorine changed everything. If Amelia had drowned in her pool and somehow ended up in the ocean, someone had moved her body. That pointed away from suicide and toward something much more deliberate. Why move her body to the beach? To make it look like an accident? And who benefited from Amelia's death, appearing accidental rather than murder?

And now he had a mystery man, Vinny with no last name, who'd had an intense private conversation with Amelia hours before her death, then left the party agitated.

Ray pulled into the station parking lot, already planning his next moves. He needed to canvass the other party guests about Vinny, run the partial name through the system, and start building a timeline of Amelia's final hours.

The case was shifting from an accident or suicide to something much more complex. Ray felt the familiar surge of energy that came with a real investigation. After three days of dead ends, he finally had leads worth pursuing.

Whoever Vinny was, Ray was going to find him and find out what he and Amelia had talked about by the pool.

14. OIL AND MOTIVE

The all-hands-on-deck phone call came at five in the morning, and Dennis was in the newsroom before six.

When he arrived, Janice, EK's assistant, handed him the copy. He sat at his desk and read the story while waiting for the rest of the staff to arrive.

Los Angeles Times–January 29, 1969

SANTA BARBARA, CA - An environmental catastrophe is unfolding off the coast of Southern California, with a massive oil spill threatening marine life and local economies. The spill began on January 28 and is rapidly becoming one of the worst environmental disasters in U.S. history.

The calamity started when Union Oil's Platform A, located about six miles off the coast of Summerland, California, experienced a blowout. Initial attempts to reseal the well proved futile as pressured oil burst through the ocean floor, creating cracks and releasing oil directly into the water. Within hours, a thick and toxic black tide began to spread, covering the once-pristine waters and beaches.

Dennis felt a knot of anger and sadness in his chest. The

beaches and wildlife weren't just scenery for him—they were part of cherished memories of a California he loved and took pride in.

With his signature glasses perched atop his head, EK slammed a paper onto the central table, drawing the room's attention.

"Listen up, everyone! I don't have to tell you how massive this story is. Santa Barbara might not be in our backyard, but this spill affects all of California. We need to address this from the Orange County perspective."

EK began handing out assignments. "Samantha, I want you to get reactions from our local environmental groups and marine biologists at UCI. Find out what this spill means for our coastlines."

He turned to a reporter with a camera hanging from his neck. "Wally, take your camera to the coast. Interview locals, fishermen, and tourists. Gauge their reactions."

"Claire, Dennis, I want a feature on the history of oil drilling in California. Let's inform our readers why this happened and what safety precautions are in place."

Finally, he looked at a couple of seasoned reporters. "Maggie, Paul, I want both of you to head up to Santa Barbara. Give us firsthand coverage. And dig into Union Oil. We need to know who's accountable."

The reporters dispersed to their assignments. Dennis watched Claire gather her research materials for the library, then made his decision. Claire could dig up the history. He needed to chase something that might still bleed—and the oil assignment gave him the perfect excuse to visit Jack Hart.

. . .

Hart Oil Company operated from a modest office complex in Corona Del Mar, not far from the Newport Beach coast. From the street, the building seemed unassuming, with a faded sign for a travel agency swinging below Jack's office window. Dennis climbed the worn stairs to the second floor, reviewing his notes. According to Carmen Montez, Jack stood to inherit half of Amelia's estate—worth over a million dollars.

The office reeked of stale cigarettes and had the cramped feel of a struggling business. Jack looked older than his early fifties. He was overweight with a pale complexion that suggested more time behind a desk than in the field. Dennis noticed the desk held business papers and an ashtray, but no family photos—odd for a married man's office.

"Mr. Hart? I'm Dennis Driver from the Daily Pilot. I'm researching the history of California oil production for background on our coverage of the Santa Barbara oil spill. I understand your father was part of that history?"

Jack's expression shifted from wariness to something approaching pride. "Yeah. Dad got his start in Newport Beach back in the late twenties. Hell of a time to be in oil around here."

"How so?"

Jack gestured toward the window overlooking the coast. "In the thirties and forties, you had a whole forest of derricks covering this coastline. Balboa Peninsula, Huntington Beach — looked like a mechanical forest. Dad always said it was like striking gold."

Dennis made notes, genuinely interested despite his ulterior motive. "What happened to all that production?"

"Played out, mostly. Some environmental pressure, too, people wanting their pretty beaches back." Jack's tone carried resentment. "By the sixties, most of the onshore wells were done. That's why they moved offshore, like this Union Oil platform that just blew up."

"Is that why your business struggled?"

Jack's face darkened. "Struggled? We didn't struggle. We adapted. Dad diversified, invested in real estate, built a solid estate for the family." He paused, his jaw tightening. "At least until Amelia got her hands on it."

Dennis felt the opening he'd been waiting for. "Your stepmother?"

"She married Dad for his money, shut out his old friends, and spent like it was Monopoly cash." Jack's bitterness was immediate and raw. "Everyone could see what she was except him."

"That must have been difficult, watching the family business assets being spent."

"Difficult doesn't begin to cover it." Jack leaned back in his chair, his resentment building. "You know what Dad used to tell me? 'Jack, this oil money is generational wealth. Take care of it, and it'll take care of your children.' Well, Amelia sure took care of it, all right."

Dennis looked up from his notes. "What do you mean?"

"Gambling. Throwing away money in Vegas, probably other places too. Dad's oil money, the money that was supposed to last generations." Jack's voice rose slightly.

"Money that should have gone to taking care of the family."

"Are you referring to anyone specific?"

"My mother. She needs daily care—early dementia. The costs are..." Jack gestured around his modest office. "Well, let's just say what's left of Hart Oil Company isn't exactly thriving."

Dennis felt the weight of what Jack was revealing. "So

Amelia's spending affected your ability to care for your mother?"

"Her gambling, her spending, her whole lifestyle." Jack caught himself, seeming to realize how much he was revealing.

"But she did inherit half his estate when he died?"

Jack's jaw tightened. "Dad set up that trust when he was thinking clearly, before she got her hooks in him completely.

If he'd known what she'd become..."

"And now with her death?"

Jack was quiet for a moment. "Now I can finally settle Dad's estate properly. Make sure his money goes where it should have gone in the first place—taking care of family, not funding some gambling addiction."

Dennis felt the conversation shifting from oil history to murder motive. "Where were you on New Year's Eve, Mr. Hart?"

"What?" Jack's attention sharpened. "Why would you ask that? I thought you were here about the oil spill."

"Just trying to get a complete picture. The timing of Amelia's death, so soon after your father's passing..."

"I was home with my mother, if you must know." Jack's tone became defensive, and the way he mentioned his mother sounded rehearsed.

"When was the last time you spoke with Amelia?"

"I don't know. Months ago, maybe? We didn't exactly chat regularly." Jack hesitated. "Though she had been asking questions about borrowing against the house, which is a trust asset." "And what did you tell her?"

Jack's expression suggested he'd refused those requests. "I told her Dad's legacy wasn't a piggy bank for her gambling debts."

Dennis closed his notebook. He had enough for now—motive, opportunity, and a man who benefited from Amelia's death. "Thank you for your time, Mr. Hart. This background on local oil production is very helpful."

"Look," Jack said as Dennis stood to leave, "I didn't like Amelia, and I won't pretend I did. But I didn't kill her, if that's what you're getting at."

"I didn't suggest you did."

"Didn't you?" Jack's eyes were hard. "Watch what you print, Mr. Driver. The personal stuff is off the record."

Dennis met his gaze. Was that a threat, or just PR damage control? He wasn't sure which answer made Jack look worse.

Walking to his car, Dennis felt the familiar excitement of a developing story. Jack Hart had a clear motive—the financial benefit of inheriting half of the estate. His alibi was his mother, and his answers about that night sounded practiced.

Back at the office, he'd write up the oil industry background for Claire's research while pursuing this lead. Jack Hart had just moved to the top of his suspect list, right alongside the mysterious Vinny that Detective Stone was hunting.

The pieces were starting to come together, and Dennis could feel the story building toward something big.

15. PERSONS OF INTEREST

Ray finished his cigarette and picked up the phone to call Julie. The autopsy addendum had changed everything—Amelia Hart's death was now officially a homicide investigation.

"Ms. Bloom, this is Detective Stone. I have some news about your mother's case. We're now investigating her death as a homicide."

He heard Julie's sharp intake of breath. "A homicide? You mean someone killed her?"

"The medical examiner found chlorine in her lungs—pool water, not ocean water. Someone moved her body after she drowned." Ray kept his voice steady, professional. "I need to ask you about someone who was at the party. A man named Vinny."

"Vinny? I don't know anyone named Vinny." Julie's confusion sounded genuine, but Ray had learned that grief could make people forget things or hide them. "There was no Vinny on the guest list. I wrote all the invitations myself."

She's either telling the truth or she's a great liar, Ray thought, making a note.

"One of the guests mentioned him. Mid-forties, well-dressed, seemed to know your mother well. They had a private conversation by the pool."

"I wasn't here, so I don't know who that could be. Mom knew a lot of people I didn't know."

Can you ask around? Check with your mother's friends, see if anyone knows about a Vinny in her life?"

"Of course. Detective, am I safe here? Should I leave the house?"

Ray hesitated. The killer had already gotten what they wanted, but Julie was the only witness to her mother's final hours. "Keep your doors locked and call me if anything feels wrong. Don't let anyone in you don't know."

After the call with Julie Bloom, Ray walked to the window, staring out at the gray January sky. The crime scene photos sat on his desk like accusations—one of Amelia Hart at a charity event just weeks before her death, smiling and radiant, completely unaware that someone in her circle was planning her murder.

The taste of black coffee had gone bitter in his mouth. Four months in Laguna Beach, and he was still adjusting to investigations where the victims had names and faces everyone recognized. In Los Angeles, dead bodies had been statistics. Here, they were neighbors.

"Detective Stone?" Sergeant O'Neil appeared in his doorframe, expression carefully neutral. "There's a reporter out here, says he has information about the Hart case. Dennis Driver from the Daily Pilot."

Ray set down his coffee cup, the ceramic clicking against the desk like a period at the end of a sentence. "Send him in."

The young man who entered didn't match Ray's expectations. Too clean-cut for a newspaper hack, too earnest for someone who'd been working the beat long enough to develop the cynical edge most reporters carried like armor. But there was something in his posture—the way he held his shoulders, the careful sweep of his eyes across the station—that spoke of military training.

"Detective Stone? Dennis Driver." The handshake was firm without being aggressive. Direct eye contact, respectful but not deferential. "I appreciate you taking the time."

Ray gestured toward the small conference room, noting how Dennis's gaze lingered on the departmental commendations on the wall. Vietnam, Ray thought. Had to be. That particular brand of awareness was the way a man looked at a room when he'd learned that safety was always temporary.

"You're new to the paper," Ray said, settling into his chair. It wasn't a question.

"Two months at the Pilot. Three months out of the Army." Dennis met his gaze steadily, no apology in his voice for either fact.

Ray leaned back, studying the reporter's face. Young, but not green. There was a weight behind his eyes that came from seeing things no twenty-three-year-old should have to see. "What makes you think there's a story here beyond what we've already told the public?"

Dennis opened his notebook with hands that weren't quite steady—not nervousness, Ray realized, but the fine tremor that sometimes lingered after too much coffee and too little sleep. The kind of shake Ray recognized in his own hands on bad mornings.

"I interviewed Amelia Hart's stepson, Jack Hart," Dennis

said, consulting his notes. "I think you might want to consider him a person of interest."

Ray kept his expression neutral, but internally, he was reassessing. The kid wasn't fishing for quotes. "Why's that?"

"He stands to inherit over a million dollars from her death. And from what I could tell, he needs the money." Dennis paused, glancing up from his notebook. "Plus, someone in the family pointed me in his direction."

"Someone in the family?" Ray leaned forward slightly. "Who?"

"Can't give up the source's name. But they seemed genuinely concerned about Jack's reaction to Amelia's political activities."

Ray felt that familiar tingle at the base of his skull—the detective instinct that said this was worth pursuing. His interviews with Julie had focused on the immediate circumstances of Amelia's death, not the longer patterns of family tension. It was exactly the kind of lead that an outsider might catch while those closest to the case missed it.

"Why bring this to me?" Ray asked. "Why not just write the story?"

Dennis closed his notebook, his expression growing serious. "Because Julie Bloom said you really listened to her concerns. And because..." He hesitated, then seemed to make a decision. "Because I've seen what happens when the truth gets buried under convenient explanations. In Vietnam, we called it 'acceptable losses.' I didn't come home to watch it happen here."

The room went quiet except for the hum of fluorescent lights and the distant sound of traffic on the coastal highway. Ray studied Dennis's face, seeing the look of a man who'd lost faith in easy answers.

"What do you want from me?"

"Information I can verify independently. Context, you might be willing to share off the record." Dennis paused. "And maybe a heads-up if you find something that changes the direction of your investigation."

It was a reasonable request, but Ray had learned to be careful about reporters. Too many LAPD investigations had been compromised by leaks to the press. Still, something about this kid felt different. Maybe it was the military bearing, or the fact that he'd brought information instead of just asking for it.

"You understand this is an active investigation," Ray said carefully. "I can't share details that might compromise our work."

"I understand. I'm not looking for a scoop. I'm looking for the truth."

Ray made a decision that surprised him. "Alright. But this works both ways. You hear something, you share it. And if I tell you something's off the record, it stays that way."

"Agreed."

As Dennis stood to leave, Ray found himself curious about something. "What made you choose journalism? After the Army, I mean."

The young man paused at the door, his expression thoughtful. "Same reason you chose police work, I imagine. Someone has to ask the hard questions. Someone has to care when the easy answers don't add up."

After Dennis left, Ray sat alone in the conference room, turning over their conversation. The kid had good instincts and seemed genuinely committed to finding the truth about Amelia Hart's death. But Ray had learned the hard way that good intentions didn't always protect people from the consequences of asking the wrong questions.

He looked out the window at the gray January sky, thinking about acceptable losses and the price of truth. For the first time since arriving in Laguna Beach, Ray felt like he might have found someone who understood that justice mattered more than convenience.

Whether that was a good thing or a dangerous thing remained to be seen.

After Dennis left, Ray stepped outside for air, letting the cool ocean breeze clear his head. Two suspects now— Vinny, the mystery man who'd had a private poolside conversation with Amelia, and Jack Hart, the bitter stepson who stood to inherit a fortune. The case reminded Ray of his own father's resentment over family money, how financial pressure could twist love into something uglier.

Back inside, he picked up the phone and dialed Jack Hart's business number.

"Hart Oil."

"Mr. Hart, this is Detective Ray Stone with Laguna Beach Police. I'm investigating Amelia Hart's death, and I'd like to speak with you."

A pause. "Has something happened? I heard it was suicide."

"We're treating it as a homicide now. I can come to your office, or you can come to the station. Your choice."

Another pause, longer this time. "I'll come to the station. Give me an hour."

While waiting, Ray called the Orange County Sheriff's Department for background information, then reviewed the case file. By the time Jack Hart arrived, Ray had a complete picture— no criminal record, business licenses current but revenues declining, multiple home nursing debts turned over to collections.

Jack Hart walked into the station looking exactly like Dennis had described—overweight, tired, defensive. Ray led him to the interview room and started the recorder.

"Mr. Hart, thank you for coming in. I'm investigating your stepmother's death, which we now know was a homicide."

Jack blinked hard, as if trying to reset what he'd just heard. "Homicide? But I thought..."

"Someone drowned her in the pool and moved her body to the beach. Where were you New Year's Eve?"

"Home with my mother." The answer came too quickly, just like Dennis had noted.

Ray leaned back, studying Jack's face. "All evening? Didn't go out at all?"

"Her night nurse quit recently, and I can't leave her alone. Too many drunk drivers." Jack shifted in his seat. "I watched the ball drop on TV, went to bed around twelve-thirty."

Something about the specificity of that detail struck Ray as odd—too precise for a casual memory. "Can your mother confirm the exact timing?"

"Yes, but you understand she has dementia." Jack's voice carried a defensive edge, but his eyes darted away for just a moment.

"Tell me about your relationship with Amelia."

"We didn't have a relationship. She married my father for his money, and everyone knew it except him."

Ray remembered his stepmother, how family money could become a battleground. "That must have been frustrating."

Jack's composure cracked. "Frustrating? She spent his money like water while my mother requires care I can barely afford."

"When did you last see Amelia?"

"Months ago. We didn't socialize." Jack paused, then seemed to catch himself. "Actually, maybe it was Christmas. No, Thanksgiving. She came by the office once, but that was back in November."

Ray made a note of the contradiction. First, months ago, then a specific holiday. "What did she want when she came to your office?"

"She was calling about borrowing against the house to pay her debts."

"And what did you tell her?"

"I told her no."

Ray continued the interview for another thirty minutes. Still, Jack stuck to his revised story—home with his mother, hadn't seen Amelia since November, didn't know anything about her death beyond what he'd heard.

After Jack left, Ray sat in the interview room, reviewing his notes. The timeline contradiction was small but significant. And that overly specific detail about going to bed at twelve-thirty felt rehearsed.

He picked up the phone to call Julie back. Time to press harder on identifying Vinny, and maybe get her thoughts on Jack's claim about the November office visit.

The case was building momentum, and Ray could feel both suspects slipping deeper into his net.

16. THE MONET IN THE CLOSET

Wolf Schmidt was stripping paint from a worthless flea market canvas when someone knocked on the studio door. The acetone-soaked paper towels would need another hour to loosen the old paint, giving him time for this interruption.

Through the narrow opening, he saw a young man in a shirt and tie, sweating despite the cool January weather. The stranger shifted nervously, clutching a small notebook and tugging at his tie like it was choking him.

"Mr. Schmidt? I'm Dennis Driver from the Orange County Tribune. I'm writing about Amelia Hart's death."

Wolf's first instinct was to close the door. Reporters meant questions, and questions were dangerous for a man in his position. "I am busy."

"The police are investigating it as a homicide now."

That stopped Wolf cold. His hand tightened on the doorframe. "Homicide? Someone has killed her?"

He stepped aside to let Dennis in, his mind racing. If Amelia had been murdered, the police would be looking at everyone in her life—including him. And with his side business in art forgery, any police attention was unwelcome.

Dennis entered the studio, his eyes immediately scanning the large space. Wolf tensed as the reporter's gaze swept across the various easels and work stations—this had been Amelia's domain, her established artist's studio that she'd generously shared with him when he first arrived in Laguna Beach three years ago.

"How well did you know Mrs. Hart?" Dennis asked, notebook ready but still glancing around.

"Very well. This was her studio—she gave me space to rent when I first came to America." Wolf gestured around the expansive room filled with natural light. "She was an established artist, very successful. She helped me to get started in restoration work."

"Were you close?"

Wolf chose his words carefully. "She was a generous mentor. When she saw my work—my ability to match the brushstrokes, to understand techniques of the masters—she was very much impressed." That was certainly true. Amelia had been amazed by his uncanny ability to replicate any artist's style, skills honed through years as a restorer in Germany.

Dennis fumbled with his pen, dropping it and having to retrieve it from the floor. "When did you last see her?"

Wolf paused, looking around the studio that still felt like it belonged to Amelia. "December 30th. She was here working on painting, and seemed excited about something. She mentioned selling some pieces from her collection."

Wolf debated telling Dennis about Amelia's specific plans —how she'd been excited about a trip to Las Vegas, where she planned to sell several paintings to private collectors who didn't ask too many questions. But revealing that would invite questions about which paintings, and why Vegas, and whether Wolf knew who the buyers were. Better to keep it vague.

Dennis looked up from his notes, his tie askew from his nervous tugging. "What kind of collection did she have?"

Wolf's pulse quickened. "Very impressive pieces. Early California Impressionists. Hassam, Edgar Payne, and Guy Rose. She had an excellent eye for quality work."

"Did she acquire them through galleries?"

This was dangerous territory. "Some, yes. Others were... private acquisitions. She knew people in the art world." Wolf watched Dennis scribble notes, hoping the reporter wouldn't pursue this line of questioning.

Dennis's gaze drifted to a landscape propped against the wall—the brushwork still slightly wet despite its supposedly vintage provenance. "Are you working on one of her pieces?"

"Restoration work," Wolf said quickly. "Small touch-ups, cleaning. Part of maintaining the collection."

"The police think she drowned in her pool and someone moved her body to the ocean," Dennis said. "Do you know anyone who might have wanted to hurt her?"

Wolf shook his head, his mind spinning. Should he mention the Vegas trip? Or that Amelia was planning to take several valuable pieces to sell to collectors there? But that would lead to questions about why she needed money so desperately, which paintings she was planning to sell, and how Wolf knew about her travel plans. Too risky.

"She was a generous woman. I cannot imagine who would want to hurt her."

"What about her gambling? Did anyone ever come here looking for her?"

"Not that I have noticed," Wolf said carefully. He'd actually seen Amelia with a man she met in Vegas, but admitting that would invite more questions about their relationship.

Dennis closed his notebook, but his eyes made one more sweep of the studio. "Thank you for your time, Mr. Schmidt. If you think of anything else..."

After Dennis left, Wolf locked the studio door and stared at the space that had been his sanctuary for three years. Maybe he should have told the reporter about Vegas, about Amelia's plans to sell paintings there. But explaining how he knew would have opened doors he couldn't afford to open.

He dialed his home number, his hands shaking slightly. "Hello?"

"Carol, it's me. I need to tell you something, and you should sit down."

"What's wrong?" His wife's voice carried instant concern.

"It is about Amelia. A reporter just left—the police think she was murdered."

Carol's sharp intake of breath carried across the line. "Murdered? But Wolf, what about your arrangement with her? If the police start investigating the studio..."

Wolf looked around the space that had given him his start in America. For two years, he'd been supplementing his restoration income by creating works for Amelia's personal collection. She'd been fascinated by his ability to replicate the brushstrokes of the California masters perfectly, and she'd commissioned several pieces to enhance her reputation as a sophisticated collector.

"The pieces in her house," Carol continued. "If they're examined closely..."

"I know this." Wolf's voice was tight. Amelia had five of his works hanging in her home—a Hassam, two Guy Rose land-scapes, an Edgar Payne mountain scene, and a William Wendt desert painting. All created to her specifications, all designed to impress her social circle and establish her credentials as a serious art collector.

"There is more," Wolf said. "She was planning to take some paintings to Las Vegas, to sell them through a connection there. She needed money for her gambling debts."

"Which paintings?"

"I do not know for certain. But Carol... what if she was planning to sell some of my work? What if the buyers discovered they were not authentic?"

The silence on the line was heavy with implications. If Amelia had been murdered because someone discovered his forgeries, Wolf was as much to blame as whoever had pushed her into that pool.

"I will be careful," he told Carol. "But we need to prepare for the possibility that this becomes very complicated."

After hanging up, Wolf walked through the studio that no longer felt safe. Five forged masterpieces hung in a dead woman's house, and he had no idea who might have discovered their secret—or whether that discovery had cost Amelia Hart her life.

17. PORTRAITS AND POLITICS

Ray's next stop was Mary Ann Fitzpatrick, another name from Julie's guest list. She lived in a beachfront cottage just a few blocks from the Hart house, and when she answered the door, her sun-bleached hair and deeply tanned skin marked her as a longtime Laguna local.

"Mrs. Fitzpatrick? Detective Stone, Laguna Beach Police. I'm investigating Amelia Hart's death."

"Of course, come in. Poor Amelia." She led him to a living room that looked like it had been decorated by the tide — shells on every surface, driftwood sculptures, gauzy curtains like sea foam. "I still can't believe she's gone. Suicide just doesn't seem like her."

"We're actually investigating it as a homicide now. I understand you were at her New Year's Eve party?"

Mary Ann's hand went to her throat. "Homicide? You mean someone killed her?"

"That's what we're trying to determine. Can you tell me about the party? Did you notice anything unusual?"

She settled into a chair across from him, her expression growing serious. "It seemed normal at first. Amelia was a good hostess, and everyone was having fun. But now that I think about it..." She paused. "There was a man there I didn't recognize."

Ray's attention sharpened. "Can you describe him?"

"Mid-forties maybe, dark hair, expensive suit. He kept to himself mostly, didn't really mingle. Someone called him Vinny, I think."

"Did you see him interact with Amelia?"

"Yes, actually. They talked privately by the pool for quite a while. It looked... intense."

Ray's pen moved quickly across his notepad. "Intense how?"

"Not angry, but serious. Like they were discussing something important." Mary Ann suddenly brightened. "Wait—I took some photos that night with my Polaroid. Let me see if I got him in any of them."

She disappeared into another room and returned with a handful of photos. Ray watched as she shuffled through snapshots of partygoers raising glasses and embracing as midnight approached.

"Here," she said, handing him a photo. "This might be your Vinny."

Ray studied the image. A dark-haired man in an expensive suit stood slightly apart from a group of celebrating guests. Even indoors at night, he wore sunglasses. Ray also noticed an expensive watch that had caught the camera flash —too flashy for someone trying to keep a low profile.

"And this one too," Mary Ann said, passing him a second photo.

This one showed the same man walking away from the camera, his back to the celebration. While everyone else was embracing and laughing, Vinny was leaving.

"These are exactly what I need," Ray said. "Can I keep them?"

"Of course. Anything to help find out what happened to Amelia."

Ray slipped the photos into his notebook. Finally, he had a face to go with the name. "Do you remember what time he left?"

"Before midnight, I think. Most of us stayed to watch the ball drop on TV, but he was gone by then."

After thanking Mary Ann for her cooperation, Ray drove the few blocks to Julie's house. She answered the door in yoga clothes, looking like she'd been in the middle of a workout.

"Sorry to interrupt your morning, Miss Bloom. I have something I'd like you to look at."

She led him into the living room, and he showed her the photos of Vinny.

Julie studied them carefully, shaking her head. "I've never seen him before. Are you sure he was at the party?"

"Multiple witnesses have confirmed it. Just one other question. Was Jack Hart at the party?"

Julie's expression hardened. "Absolutely not. Mom wouldn't have invited him, and he wouldn't have come if she had."

"Why's that?"

"They didn't get along. Jack always resented her marriage to his father, thought she was a gold digger." Julie sat down heavily. "Detective, I need to tell you something. Jack and my mother were at opposite ends politically."

Ray looked up from his notes, sensing this was important.

"Jack is active in the John Birch Society, while Mom was anti-war, supported civil rights, and women's liberation."

Ray had dealt with political extremists before, knew how ideology could twist family disputes into something dangerous. "Did this cause problems between them?"

"More than problems. Jack actually accused Mom of being a communist." Julie's voice carried old frustration.

"What did your mother think about that?"

"She was scared, honestly. Jack thought her political art was dangerous, un-American." Julie paused, as if remembering something painful. "Detective, now that I think about it, Mom had been getting threatening notes in the mail. Someone calling her a communist sympathizer, threatening to 'shut her up.'"

A prickle of urgency climbed Ray's spine. He'd worked a case in his previous department where political harassment had escalated to violence. A union organizer was beaten nearly to death by extremists. The cruelty of people who hid behind ideology while terrorizing their neighbors never ceased to disgust him.

"When did these start?"

"A few months ago. Some came in the mail, others were pinned to our gate. Mom thought Jack or his John Birch.

Society friends might be behind them."

"Do you think she kept any of these notes?"

"Possibly. She was worried enough to save them, in case she needed to go to the police." Julie met his eyes, and Ray could see the remorse of not reporting the threats earlier. "Detective, I don't want to believe it, but... if someone did this because of her art, because of her politics, Jack's the first person I'd suspect."

"I'm looking at everyone who had motive and opportunity.

Can you search for those notes? They could be important evidence."

"I'll look through her papers this afternoon."

W alking back to his car, Ray reviewed two major developments: photos of the mysterious Vinny and evidence that Amelia had been receiving political threats, possibly connected to Jack Hart.

Sitting in his unmarked Ford, Ray reconsidered Dennis Driver, the young reporter who'd brought him the Jack Hart lead. Maybe the kid could be trusted. Jack's financial motive and family resentment, mixed with ideological hatred, were a dangerous combination.

Ray started the engine, his mind already planning the next steps. He needed to show Vinny's photo to other party guests, search for those threatening notes, and take a much closer look at Jack Hart's political connections.

The case was building momentum, and for the first time since Amelia's body was discovered, Ray felt like he was closing in on her killer.

18. POLITICAL ART

Dennis arrived at the Fields Gallery to find competing demonstrations on opposite ends of the street. One group carried signs reading *COMMIE SYMPATHIZER* and *SUPPORT OUR TROOPS*, while counter-protesters held *END THE WAR* and *BRING OUR BOYS HOME* placards. The tension was palpable, a physical manifestation of the controversy surrounding Amelia's work.

Inside, the gallery buzzed with conversation around Amelia Hart's controversial political paintings. Dennis spotted Julie Bloom talking with gallery owner William Fields and Wolf Schmidt near a large canvas titled "War's End"—a stark depiction of wounded soldiers returning home, life-sized figures rendered in ash grays and blood browns, their faces hollow with exhaustion. The painting dominated the main wall, impossible to ignore, impossible to look at without feeling something.

He waited until Julie detached from the two men to approach. "Hello, Miss Bloom."

Julie's expression grew cautious as she recognized Dennis as the reporter who had previously interviewed her at home.

"I hoped I might ask you a few questions about your mother's recent work." Dennis gestured toward the paintings. "These seem to have generated strong reactions."

"Too strong," Julie said, glancing toward the windows where the protesters' chants could be heard. "Mom knew her political art was controversial, but she felt she had to speak out."

"Did the controversy ever become personal? Threatening?"

Julie's jaw tightened, and she glanced toward the door before answering. "Yes, she'd been getting hostile calls. People were saying terrible things—calling her a traitor, saying she is dishonoring soldiers. It escalated after the Times piece about her new work."

"Did she take the threats seriously?"

"She tried not to let them intimidate her. But yes, they worried her."

Dennis filed the information away, watching Julie's face carefully. There was something she wasn't saying, a hesitation in her answers. Before he could probe further, she excused herself to greet arriving guests.

The gallery was filling with afternoon visitors—a mix of serious collectors, curious locals, and what appeared to be art students from the college. Dennis positioned himself near "War's End," observing the reactions. Some viewers stood in contemplative silence. Others moved quickly past, their discomfort visible. One older man muttered something to his wife about "disrespectful propaganda" before leaving entirely.

When Wolf Schmidt stepped outside for a smoke, Dennis followed. The artist stood near the gallery's side entrance, away from the protesters, lighting a cigarette with hands that weren't quite steady.

Dennis approached and offered him a light, though Wolf's cigarette was already lit. The artist accepted anyway, a small acknowledgment of the gesture.

"Mr. Schmidt, I interviewed you about Mrs. Hart's death."

Wolf nodded carefully, exhaling smoke toward the ocean.

"I'm trying to understand the climate around her work. The hostility seems intense."

"She knew her work angered people." Wolf gestured toward the protesters across Coast Highway. "That's just the visible part. There were others, less public in their opposition."

"What do you mean, less public?"

Wolf hesitated, studying Dennis as if weighing how much to say. "Men in suits. At openings, watching. Not buying, not talking to artists. Just... present. Amelia noticed them, too."

Dennis felt his pulse quicken. "Did she ever mention feeling surveilled? Phone calls that seemed off?"

Wolf's expression darkened. "She mentioned it was getting to her, the pressure. Said once that she'd heard strange clicks on her line, but then laughed it off, said she was being para-noid." He paused. "Another time she mentioned thinking someone had been in her studio when she was away. Nothing taken, but things... not quite where she'd left them."

"When was this?"

"Two, three weeks before she died. But she wasn't certain—said it was probably nothing, that she was letting the political tension get to her. She mentioned it more than once, though, like she was trying to convince herself."

They stood in silence for a moment, watching fog begin to roll in from the ocean. The protesters' voices seemed distant now, muffled by the marine layer.

"Did you tell the police about this?"

"I told them what I knew." Wolf dropped his cigarette and crushed it beneath his heel. "Whether they listened is another matter." He turned toward the door, then paused. "Be careful with this, Driver. People who ask the wrong questions sometimes attract the wrong kind of attention."

B ack inside the gallery, Dennis scanned the crowd, cataloging potential interview subjects—collectors who might have known Amelia, other artists who could speak to the political climate. That's when he noticed a man who didn't fit the pattern.

While everyone else in the gallery moved, circulated, engaged with the art or each other, this man stood apart—a man in a dark suit, late thirties, standing near the back wall with the stillness of someone trained to watch without being noticed.

The man wasn't looking at the paintings. His eyes moved systematically across the crowd, pausing on faces, cataloging. He held a small notepad, occasionally making brief notations. When Dennis shifted position to get a better view, the man's gaze moved to meet his.

The look was professional, assessing, flat. The kind of look Dennis had seen in Saigon—intelligence officers, CIA, the various flavors of government surveillance. Recognition passed between them: I see you seeing me.

Dennis studied him more carefully now. The conservative haircut, the way he stood with his weight balanced, ready to move. The suit was good quality but generic—nothing that would make him memorable. He positioned himself with clear sightlines to both gallery exits and the main cluster of controversial paintings.

As Dennis watched, the man spoke briefly with William Fields near the gallery office. Fields seemed to know him—they exchanged a few words, Fields nodding, the man making another note. Then the suited man moved toward the door, passing within a few feet of Dennis.

Up close, Dennis noticed more: polished shoes with thick soles, the kind favored by people who might need to move quickly. No wedding ring. A slight bulge under the left arm that could be a shoulder holster or just the way his jacket hung. The man gave Dennis a brief, neutral glance—acknowledging he'd been observed—and stepped outside.

Through the window, Dennis watched him walk past the protesters without acknowledging them, get into an unmarked sedan—late model Ford, dark blue—and drive away.

Not staying to view art. Not interested in making a purchase. Just observation, documentation, and departure.

He found Julie again near the gallery office. "Miss Bloom," he said quietly, "has anyone else been asking questions about your mother's work? Government officials, perhaps?"

Julie's eyes widened slightly. "What do you mean, government officials?"

"Your mother's political work made her visible to certain interests. Anti-war artists have drawn federal attention before." Dennis kept his voice low. "It's worth considering all possibilities."

"I... I don't know anything about that." Julie glanced around the gallery, suddenly nervous. "Detective Stone is handling the investigation. I think you should coordinate with him rather than pursuing this on your own."

Dennis nodded, understanding her caution. She was frightened now—the idea of government involvement had clearly unsettled her. But whether that fear came from knowledge or simply the suggestion itself, he couldn't tell.

As he left the gallery, passing between the dueling protesters outside, Dennis felt the pieces beginning to align. The threatening calls. Wolf's observations about surveillance at previous openings. Amelia's suspicions about her phone, her studio. And now, concrete evidence that someone official was monitoring the gallery and its visitors.

By the time Dennis reached his car, the afternoon had given way to early evening, fog rolling thick off the ocean. Through the gray haze, the gallery lights blazed, illuminating the controversial paintings inside.

Dennis sat for a moment, organizing his thoughts. He opened his notebook and reviewed what he'd gathered:

Julie confirmed political threats against Amelia—escalating, personal, and designed to intimidate.

Wolf had noticed surveillance at previous openings. Amelia had suspected her phone was compromised, and her studio was searched. She'd been uncertain, yes, but the concerns were persistent enough that she'd mentioned them multiple times.

Dennis had seen it himself tonight—the man in the suit, professional surveillance, documentation, the meeting with Fields that suggested official business rather than casual attendance.

Individually, these might be a coincidence. Together, they formed a pattern.

Dennis started the car. He needed to check the Times' morgue files, see if other anti-war artists had received threats or experienced surveillance. The federal angle was worth pursuing. Political silencing and government surveillance felt like the real story beneath the surface. Someone needed to ask the harder questions about who might have wanted Amelia Hart silenced.

He pulled out onto Coast Highway, headlights cutting through the gathering fog. His reporter's instinct told him to keep digging, no matter where it led.

Behind him, the gallery lights faded into the gray evening, and the sound of protesters dissolved into the muffled quiet of the fog.

19. ERASING THE ARTIST

Sergeant O'Neal was dusting the door for fingerprints when Detective Ray Stone arrived at the Fields Gallery. Uniformed officers secured the scene, while gallery owner William Fields stood nearby, looking shaken.

"What happened here?" Ray asked.

"Break-in sometime after midnight," O'Neal reported. "No sign of forced entry.. Clean job.."

Ray turned to Fields. "What's missing?"

"Just one painting. Amelia Hart's 'War's End.'" Fields gestured toward an empty frame on the gallery wall. "Cut right out of the frame with a razor or sharp knife."

Ray examined the frame closely. The cuts were precise, surgical even.. "Who has keys to the gallery?"

"Myself, my assistant Fiona, and the overnight cleaning crew from Coastal Services."

"I'm gonna need their contact information." Ray studied the empty frame, his mind already working through possibilities. *Either the thief had a key, or he hid inside after closing..*" Was this painting particularly valuable?"

Fields ran a hand through his hair. "It was Amelia's last

completed work. It got a lot of attention because it was politi-cally controversial, but in terms of market value..." He shrugged. "I had no serious offers for it yet."

Ray felt the familiar tingle of pieces starting to connect. "Mr. Fields, I'm investigating Amelia Hart's murder. Do you think this theft could be connected?"

"Murder?" Fields froze, his voice dropping to a rasp. "I thought... I mean, everyone said it was suicide."

"We're treating it as a homicide. So I need to ask—who else knew about this painting? Who might have wanted it destroyed or stolen?"

"No. I have no idea.

D ennis Driver approached from across the street.
"Detective Stone? I heard about the break-in. I think this might be connected to what we discussed yesterday."

Ray stepped outside the crime scene tape. "You mean Jack Hart and the political threats?"

"Exactly. That painting was the focus of the protests yester-day. Anti-war imagery that really angered the John Birch Society crowd." Dennis pulled out his notebook. "What if someone killed Amelia to silence her, and now they're trying to destroy her work?"

Ray lit a cigarette, the pieces of the case shifting in his mind like a puzzle finding its shape. It made more sense than random art theft. "You're thinking organized political motivation?"

"Look at the timing. Amelia gets threatening notes, then she's murdered, then her most controversial painting disap-pears." Dennis gestured toward the gallery. "This wasn't about money—it was about the message."

Ray inhaled deeply, wondering if Dennis was seeing a conspiracy where there was simply a coincidence. But the clean, professional nature of the theft suggested someone with resources and planning. "Tell me about these threats again. Julie said her mother thought Jack Hart might be involved."

"Jack Hart's very active in the local John Birch Society chapter. They've been vocal about artists they consider 'communist sympathizers.' Amelia's anti-war paintings put her right in their crosshairs."

"Any names besides Jack Hart?"

Dennis flipped through his notes. "I haven't identified specific individuals yet, but the John Birch Society has been organizing letter-writing campaigns against what they call 'subversive art' in Orange County galleries."

This was a concrete lead he could investigate. "If you come up with a list of names. I'd like to see it. Particularly anyone with connections to Jack Hart."

"I'll do that. But Detective..." Dennis lowered his voice. "At the gallery opening yesterday, I saw a man in a suit who didn't fit. He wasn't looking at the art—he was watching the people. Government type, maybe federal."

Ray's cigarette paused halfway to his lips. "You think federal agents are involved?"

"I don't know. But if Amelia's political art attracted the wrong kind of attention..."

"Let's not get ahead of ourselves," Ray said, though doubt crept in. Was he dealing with family hatred, organized extremists, or something even larger? "Right now, I'm focused on Jack Hart and his political associates. That's a concrete lead we can pursue."

Ray turned back to Fields. "I need to see your visitor log from yesterday, and I want to interview your staff about anyone who seemed overly interested in that particular painting."

"Of course. Whatever you need."

As Fields went to get the information, Ray reviewed his growing list of suspects. Jack Hart had financial and possibly political motives, the mysterious Vinny from the New Year's Eve party. Wolf Schmidt, with his nervous evasions and access to Amelia's work. And now, possibly an organized group targeting Amelia for her political art.

"Dennis, I want you to coordinate with me on this John Birch Society angle, but carefully. If we're dealing with organized political violence, I don't want you walking into something dangerous."

"Understood."

Ray crushed his cigarette under his heel. The art theft had opened up a new dimension to Amelia Hart's murder. Someone was trying to erase her voice permanently.

First, they took her life. Now they were coming for her legacy.

The question was whether it was her politically extreme stepson acting alone, or something larger and more organized.

Ray intended to find out.

20. BIGGER THAN A BYLINE

Dennis flattened his notes like a gambler laying down losing cards. The gallery theft, Jack Hart, the threats—they were all here, but still missing the final picture.

"So what's your theory?" EK asked, studying the timeline Dennis had constructed.

"I think Amelia Hart was killed for her political art, and now someone's trying to destroy the evidence." Dennis pointed to his notes. "But here's what Detective Stone doesn't know yet. Jack Hart's financial situation is worse than anyone realized."

EK's eyebrows rose. "How much worse?"

"I did some digging after our last conversation. Hart Oil Company hasn't just been struggling—they're hemorrhaging money. Hart owes back taxes, his mother's nursing service is threatening to sue for non-payment, and he took out a second mortgage on his house last month."

"So the inheritance isn't just attractive—it's essential for survival."

"Exactly. And that's not the half of it." Dennis pulled out a photocopied document. "I found Hart's name on a John Birch

Society fundraising letter from last October. He donated five hundred dollars he couldn't afford, which tells me he's deeply committed to their cause."

EK leaned forward. 'Dennis, half the people in Newport are Birchers. You're on the wrong track there. I'd stick with the financial motive, a man who's desperate for money. might kill to get it."

"There's more. The mystery man I saw at the gallery? I think I've seen him before." Dennis's stomach turned—not from fear exactly, but from the queasy thrill of proximity to something dangerous. "Three months ago, I covered a protest at UC Irvine where anti-war demonstrators were arrested.

Same build, same posture. He was observing then, too."

"You think he's a federal agent?

"FBI, maybe. Which means Amelia Hart might have been on someone's watch list."

"What does Detective Stone think about your federal agent theory?"

"I haven't told him yet. Wanted to run it by you first."

EK's expression grew serious. "Dennis, how deep do you want to go on this? If Hart and his political friends are involved in murder, and if federal agents are watching antiwar activists, this isn't just a crime story anymore. This becomes an investigation into surveillance and political violence."

The weight of that settled on Dennis's shoulders. "I can handle it."

"Maybe. But here's the deal—you check in with me every day. You don't go anywhere alone after dark. And if things get genuinely dangerous, we pull back."

Dennis nodded, but as he headed for the door, he wondered if he'd already crossed a line he couldn't uncross. The man at the gallery had been evaluating, cataloging. And if

Dennis was right about federal surveillance of political activists, that man might already know exactly who Dennis Driver was and what he was investigating.

The smart move would be to stick to the safe angle—Jack Hart's financial desperation and family resentment. But Dennis would never get a big story by playing it safe.

He thought about Amelia Hart, silenced for speaking truth through her art. Someone had to tell her story, even if it meant walking into the shadows where dangerous people operated.

Especially then.

21. THE NOTE

Julie sat in Emily Worthmann's office, watching the accountant sort through her mother's financial documents. The box of papers looked chaotic—bank statements, receipts, and invoices poking out at odd angles —but Emily's methodical approach was reassuring.

"I've done your mother's taxes for ten years," Emily said, making neat stacks on her desk. She adjusted her reading glasses with a familiar gesture, like she'd done this ritual countless times. "She was a lovely woman, but not great with money management."

"How bad is it?" Julie asked, dreading the answer.

Emily poured herself coffee and offered Julie a cup. "Her biggest problem was treating tax deductions like free money. She overspent on travel and entertainment, thinking the business deductions meant she could spend whatever she wanted." Emily shook her head with the weary expression of someone who'd given this lecture many times. "Your mother once told me she thought the IRS was bluffing about penalties. I assured her they weren't."

Julie nodded, feeling a flush of embarrassment. She'd been away at college, focused on her own life.

"Most of this is what I expected," Emily continued, sorting papers. "Credit card debt, overdue bills, some questionable business expenses. But here's something I haven't seen before."

She unfolded a legal document and placed it carefully in front of Julie. "A promissory note. Your mother borrowed forty thousand dollars using the house as collateral."

The floor seemed to tilt beneath Julie as she read the document. "Forty thousand? When did this happen?"

"Four months ago, according to the date."

"I had no idea." Julie's voice came out sharper than she intended, anger mixing with shock. "Mom never said a word about borrowing money against the house." *How could she risk our home without telling me?*

"Julie, this is serious. You can't sell the house or borrow against it until this lien is paid."

The betrayal hit Julie like a physical blow. "Who's the lender?"

Emily checked the document. "Vincent Di Nuccio. There's a Las Vegas address."

Julie's breath caught. "Vincent Di Nuccio? Are you sure?"

"Yes, why? Do you know him?"

Julie's mind raced. Detective Stone had been looking for a man named Vinny who was at her mother's New Year's Eve party. Vincent Di Nuccio—that had to be him. "I need to use your phone."

"Of course, but Julie, are you all right? You look like you've seen a ghost."

Julie dialed the police station with trembling fingers. "Detective Stone, please. This is Julie Bloom. It's urgent."

While she waited to be connected, Julie studied the promissory note again. But wait—how had her mother even been able to do this? "Emily, my stepbrother said the house is in a trust. Could Mom actually borrow against it?"

Emily frowned, adjusting her glasses again. "That's... complicated. If she were the trustee, she might have had some authority, but borrowing against trust property usually requires specific permissions or court approval."

"So this might not even be legal?"

"It's possible the lender didn't do proper due diligence. Or..." Emily hesitated.

"Or what?"

"Or your mother misrepresented her authority. That would be fraud."

Julie felt sick. Had her mother committed fraud on top of everything else?

"Miss Bloom? What can I do for you?"

"Detective, I'm at my mother's accountant's office. We found a promissory note. Mom borrowed forty thousand dollars from Vincent Di Nuccio. Is that the Vinny you've been looking for?"

There was a pause. "Vincent Di Nuccio? You're sure about the name?"

"I'm holding the document right now. Vincent Di Nuccio, with a Las Vegas address. Detective, is this the same person who was at the party?"

"I need to see that document immediately. Where are you?"

Julie gave him Emily's address and hung up..

"The police think this Vincent guy could be connected to your mother's death?" Emily asked quietly.

"Possibly." Julie's anger was building alongside her fear. "The police are looking for him as a person of interest." The thought that her mother died because of gambling debts made her furious. But doubt crept in, too. Had Jack really known nothing about this loan? He'd seemed genuinely surprised, but then again, Julie was learning that everyone in her family had been keeping secrets.

"Julie, I know this is overwhelming," Emily said gently. "But we need to go through the rest of these papers. If your mother owed money to dangerous people, you need to know exactly what you're dealing with."

Julie nodded, forcing herself to focus. Detective Stone would be here soon, and she wanted to have as much information as possible. Her mother's financial secrets had already cost Amelia her life. Julie wasn't going to let them destroy what remained of their family.

Twenty minutes later, Detective Stone arrived with another officer. Julie handed him the promissory note and watched his expression grow grim as he read it.

"This gives us Vincent Di Nuccio's full name and address," he said. "We can finally track down your mystery guest."

"Do you think he killed her?" Julie asked.

Detective Stone folded the document carefully. "I think your mother owed a lot of money to someone who came to her party uninvited. Whether that led to murder, we'll find out."

As the detectives left with copies of the financial documents, Julie remained in Emily's office, overwhelmed by the scope of her mother's deception. She'd been mourning the loss of a woman she thought she knew. Now she had to grieve for the mother who'd been risking everything they had.

22. DEBT AND MOTIVE

Dennis sat in the Laguna Beach police station, waiting for Detective Stone.

Ray appeared with a file folder and a cup of coffee. "Sorry to keep you waiting. I've been on the phone with the Las Vegas PD and the FBI about the Vincent Di Nuccio lead."

"FBI?"

Ray opened the folder and spread out several documents. "Vincent 'Vinny' Di Nuccio, age 44. He's not just some loan shark, Dennis. He's a made man in the Chicago outfit and manages the Stardust Casino for mob interests in Vegas. Very smooth operator—expensive suits, legitimate business front, but with connections that go all the way back to the Midwest families."

Dennis leaned forward, studying the papers. The scope of what they were dealing with suddenly felt much larger. "So when Amelia borrowed money from him..."

"She wasn't just getting a loan from some shark. She was doing business with organized crime." Ray's expression was grim. "And here's the interesting part—he flew into Orange

County on December 30th, returned to Las Vegas on January. 2nd. That puts him here during the murder window."

"Have you been able to question him?"

Ray's face darkened. "That's where it gets complicated. Vegas PD wanted to handle it. He's got a team of expensive lawyers. Claims he was in California on legitimate casino business, says the loan to Amelia was a private investment in her art career."

Dennis felt his stomach sink. "So we can't tie him to the murder?"

"Not yet. His attorneys are painting him as a respectable businessman who happened to know the victim." Ray sat back in his chair. "But here's what bothers me—a guy with Di Nuccio's reputation doesn't personally fly cross-country to collect forty thousand dollars. He's got people for that."

"Unless it wasn't about collecting the money."

"Exactly. Maybe it was about sending a message. Or maybe Amelia knew something that made her dangerous."

Dennis paused, weighing his words. "Ray, what if we're in over our heads here? If Di Nuccio is connected to the Chicago mob, this isn't just a local murder case anymore."

Ray studied him for a moment. "You having second thoughts?"

"I keep thinking about Julie, how this investigation is putting her at risk. If we're dealing with organized crime..." Dennis trailed off, the implications sinking in.

"The chlorine in Amelia's lungs says someone killed her," Ray said firmly. "Whether it was mob business, family greed, or politics, someone wanted Amelia Hart dead."

Dennis felt overwhelmed by the complexity. "So we have Di Nuccio—a mob-connected casino manager who lent Amelia forty thousand dollars. Jack Hart, who thinks he's a patriot saving America from communists. And Wolf Schmidt, who's lying about something."

"Plus, the art theft from the gallery. Someone wanted that political painting destroyed." Ray stood up. "One of these bastards is going to break. They always do.

Dennis closed his notebook, feeling the weight of the investigation. "You think Julie's safe?"

I've got a patrol car doing extra drives past her house," Ray said. "But Dennis? If this gets ugly, you call me immediately. Don't try to be a hero."

As they left the conference room, Dennis wondered if he'd already crossed that line. He was no longer just reporting on a local crime story—he was investigating organized crime, political terrorism, and murder. And somewhere in the bright afternoon sunshine, someone was walking around free, knowing exactly how Amelia Hart died and thinking they'd gotten away with it.

The thought definitely should have scared him more than it did.

23. SOMETHING TO PROTECT

Ray woke to the smell of coffee and the sound of Maggie moving quietly around her small kitchen.

Through the thin walls of the beach cottage, the thud of sneakers and the scrape of a skateboard against the wall told Ray that Willy was getting ready for school.

"Morning," Maggie whispered, handing him a cup.

Before Ray could respond, Willy appeared in the doorway, fully dressed but hair still askew from sleep. "I'm hungry."

"Okay," Maggie said. "We'll be ready to go in five minutes."

Willy studied Ray with the directness only kids possessed. "You ever get scared doing your job?"

Ray paused, thinking about standing over Amelia Hart's body, the way Julie's voice had trembled when she talked about her mother. "Sometimes. But that's normal. Being scared can keep you sharp."

Willy nodded as if this made perfect sense. "Mom gets scared when she has to deal with drunk tourists."

"Willy," Maggie warned gently, checking her reflection in the toaster's chrome surface. Her red hair was already pinned back, ready for the bandana that completed her Jolly Rigger uniform.

"What? It's true." Willy grabbed his backpack. "Ray, you ready? I want hash browns."

Ray liked his mornings with Maggie and her son Willy. Two months in, and he was still learning their rhythm—the way Maggie could transform from sleepy girlfriend to efficient single mother in minutes, how Willy asked questions that cut straight to the heart of things.

"Let me grab my keys," Ray said, watching Maggie tie the white peasant blouse that made her look like she'd stepped off a pirate ship. The costume was ridiculous, but she wore it with dignity.

She kissed his cheek as she headed for the door. "See you boys at the JR."

The drive to the Jolly Rigger took ten minutes through Laguna's winding streets. Willy chattered about a history test while Ray navigated the morning traffic, tourists already claiming parking spots near the beach.

"You think pirates were actually cool?" Willy asked as they pulled into the restaurant's lot. "Or just, like, smelly criminals?"

"Probably smelly criminals," Ray said. "Most criminals are pretty disappointing in real life."

The Jolly Rigger sat on a prime corner overlooking the ocean, its weathered wood exterior and skull-and-crossbones flag making it look like a theme park attraction. Inside, the pirate motif continued with rope nets, treasure chests, and faded nautical maps covering the walls.

Maggie emerged from the kitchen carrying a coffeepot, her

uniform complete now with the red bandana and black vest that emphasized her curves. She moved between tables, refilling cups and taking orders with a smile that never seemed forced.

"Ahoy, mateys," she said when she reached their booth, slipping into character for Willy's benefit. "What can this humble wench bring ye this fine morning?"

Willy giggled. "Hash browns. Extra crispy."

"Scrambled eggs and wheat toast," Ray added, still getting used to being served by his girlfriend while her coworkers watched.

"Aye aye, captain." Maggie winked at Ray before heading back to the kitchen.

Willy pulled out a comic book, but Ray noticed him keeping one eye on the other customers, the way kids do when they're comfortable in a space but still aware. This was Willy's second home—the place he came after school while his mom finished her shift.

"She's good at this," Ray observed.

"Yeah," Willy said without looking up from his comic. "She takes care of people. That's just what she does."

It was a simple statement, but it hit Ray harder than he expected. After months of taking care of only himself, of trusting no one, he was learning what it felt like to be part of something bigger than his own careful solitude.

I n the unmarked sedan, Wil was fascinated by the radio chatter and the emergency equipment. "Do you carry a gun?"

"Yes, but it's not a toy. It's a tool for protecting people."

"Do you think you'll have to use it on this case?"

Ray thought about Di Nuccio's reputation, the mob connections. "I hope not. The goal is always to solve things without anyone getting hurt."

At Top of the World School, Wil grabbed his skateboard and backpack. "You can call me Will. Mom is the only one who calls me Willy."

"Okay, Will. You can call me Ray."

"I might call you Detective sometimes around my friends." Wil grinned. "Sounds cooler."

As Will ran toward the school entrance, Ray's radio crackled again. "Detective Stone, FBI Agent Morrison is waiting in Conference Room B. Says it's urgent regarding the Di Nuccio case."

Ray keyed the mic. "En route. ETA five minutes."

Driving toward the station, Ray felt the Amelia Hart case settling on his shoulders differently now. Vincent Di Nuccio wasn't just another suspect—he was a mob-connected killer who represented everything Ray had sworn to protect people from. The image of Amelia Hart's body flashed through his mind, followed immediately by Wil's trusting face, asking if he ever got scared.

The radio crackled with routine traffic, but Ray's mind was on the FBI briefing waiting for him. Whatever Agent Morrison had to say about Di Nuccio's Chicago connections, Ray was ready to hear it.

It wasn't just a case anymore. It was a promise—to Maggie, to Wil, and himself—that danger wouldn't come knocking without meeting him first.

24. THE CONFIDENCE GAME

Wolf checked his rearview mirror again before opening the newspaper. Detective Stone's unmarked sedan was nowhere to be seen, but Wolf had learned to assume he was always being watched.

The Times felt heavier—not from the paper, but the lie it carried. Three carefully placed articles about Carol's "discovery" of a lost Kleitsch painting. If the police were monitoring him, they were about to watch him become wealthy.

He unfolded the paper to the Arts section, and there it was—the story that would make or break everything.

Los Angeles Times - April 13, 1969

Lost Kleitsch Painting Discovered in Pasadena Attic

A painting by notable artist Joseph Kleitsch was unexpectedly discovered in the attic of Pasadena resident Carol Ward. The work, found inside an old wooden crate, is believed to be an original oil painting by Kleitsch, renowned for his contributions to the California art scene of the early twentieth century.

The newly discovered painting, 'The Farm,' depicts Laguna pioneer Joe Thurston's historic homestead. Untouched by time, this piece provides a glimpse into the artist's vision of early Orange County.

The revelation of this artwork has caused excitement among art enthusiasts and historians. As the art community anticipates the public display of 'The Farm,' there is speculation about the painting's potential value, which could reach six figures.

Wolf smiled despite himself. Every detail was perfect.

B ack home, Carol was waiting by the window, her face tense with worry. "Did you get it?" she asked.

Wolf showed her the article, along with similar stories in the Register and Daily Pilot. "Think about the excitement these will create for our gallery showing."

Carol's hands trembled slightly. "Amelia had always hated this kind of scheme—called it "poisoning the well of art."

"Carol, we have been over this a hundred times. A lost masterpiece found by chance. With a local angle. Everyone will love the story."

Carol searched his eyes. "And if we're wrong?"

"We will not be wrong. Once people see the painting, they will be too caught up in the discovery story."

The phone's ring cut through their conversation. Wolf grabbed it quickly. "Hello." Wolf smiled and covered the mouthpiece, "It's Fields. He read the article."

"Yes, we have the Times and the Register. It's a great article. Couldn't be better."

"This is just what the gallery needed after losing Amelia's work. Great timing," Fields said.

Wolf's grip tightened on the phone. *Why would Fields*

connect Carol's discovery to Amelia's death? "The timing is... good, yes."

"I've been in this business long enough to recognize opportunity when I see it," Fields said. "I'm already getting calls from collectors. Amazing how a 'lost masterpiece' generates more interest than those political paintings that caused so much trouble."

Wolf felt his pulse quicken. Fields was being too specific, too knowing. Did he suspect the Kleitsch was forged? Or worse—did he know it was?

"I am pleased there is interest," Wolf said neutrally.

Fields' hearty laugh seemed forced. "Interest? Wolf, we're going to be the talk of the art world. I think we should arrange a private viewing before the public showing. Build anticipation. Exclusivity is key."

"That sounds... wise."

"I'll start making calls. We'll have collectors lined up at our door." Fields paused. "You know, Wolf, this kind of discovery requires careful handling. Complete discretion. I hope we understand each other."

Wolf had heard threats before. This one wore a smile and a tie.

After hanging up, Wolf stared at the phone. Carol moved closer, reading his expression. "What is wrong?"

"Nothing. William doesn't suspect anything. He's excited about the painting, knows it will be very profitable." Wolf's eyes hardened. "If he does suspect anything, he's playing the same game we are."

Carol looked at the newspaper article again, her voice barely a whisper. "What now?"

Wolf stood, his decision made. "Now we prepare for the showing. And we watch William very carefully. If he knows about the forgery, we find out what he wants."

Outside, a car drove slowly past their house. Wolf moved to the window and watched it disappear around the corner. It could have been anyone. It could have been police surveillance.

Either way, they were committed now. The articles were published, Fields was making calls, and collectors would soon be demanding to see the "lost" Kleitsch masterpiece.

He was running the biggest con of his life—while being watched for something he might not have done. Yet.

25. THE FARM AND THE FACADE

Julie wheeled her car to a stop on Ocean Street, a block short of the Fields Gallery. She got out. The evening air had a nip, a reminder that the sun had clocked out. The gallery glowed, its lights a warm spot in the creeping dusk.

She dug into her purse and fished until she found the stiff paper invite. 'The Farm,' it said in fancy letters over a picture of a painting that looked like you could walk right into it and pick an apple.

The house had been too quiet tonight, filled with the kind of silence that made her think too much about Mom's files still scattered across the kitchen table. She was looking for a little noise, a jostle of people who didn't know about her bigger problems and only wanted a smile and a nod. So, as she approached the Fields Gallery, she took a second, let her shoulders drop, and rearranged her face into something that looked ready to meet the world. Then Julie stepped over the gallery's threshold, leaving the quiet street behind her.

Inside, the gallery buzzed with voices stacked on each other. The delicate chime of glasses kissing and a string quartet sawing away in the corner wrapped the whole place in a sound blanket. Julie slipped into it, grateful for the distraction from thoughts that had been circling like vultures all day.

She sidestepped through the clots of the crowd. The electric air was thick with the smell of money and wine and a good smear of gossip. She let her ears tune into the symphony of social niceties. At the same time, her trained eye—her art history education and photography had taught her to observe, and her mother's murder had taught her to be suspicious—catalogued the players.

Carol's lips curved in a smile that drew folks like sugar. But something about her performance felt rehearsed tonight, the way she positioned herself just so beside the featured painting. Julie had known Carol since her preteen summers as a junior lifeguard, and this polished version felt like watching someone play a role.

Wolf leaned back against the wall, a glass in his hand. His way of looking at you could make you feel picked out and special—Julie had seen that charm work on others, had felt its pull herself. But tonight, she noticed how his eyes kept cutting over to 'The Farm,' like a stage manager monitoring his production. The same quality that had made Mom trust the wrong person, that easy confidence that masked calculation.

After Mom's mistakes, Julie promised herself she'd pay attention to warning signs. Wolf's performance tonight—because that's what it was—confirmed every instinct that had been telling her to keep her distance.

William Fields held court near the center of the gallery, a man who knew his power lay as much in the spectacle as in the art he sold. His voice boomed, his hands painted the air, and people circled him like planets. But when he thought no one was watching, his gaze got sharp, and he looked like he was adding sums in his head.

Off to the side, a little away from the main hustle, an old sepia photo had been propped up on an easel, a window to the past. It showed a young woman in a ladder-backed chair, a painting looming like a silent sentinel behind her. Julie moved closer, her photography training automatically cataloguing details. The photo quality, the clothing, the composition—everything screamed authenticity. But as she studied the woman's face, something cold settled in her stomach.

Carol appeared beside her, and it was like someone turned on the lights. Her smile was wide, perfectly practiced. "Thank you for coming, Julie. I'm still pinching myself."

Julie's eyes flicked between Carol and the sepia image. The resemblance wasn't just striking—it was impossible. Identical bone structure, identical eyes, identical expression. In her media studies courses, she'd learned about photo manipulation, but more importantly, she'd learned about deception from her mother's case.

"That picture of your grandmother is remarkable," Julie said carefully. "The resemblance is... extraordinary. Is she still around?"

Julie caught the half-second delay before Carol spoke. The sadness that followed was just a little too rehearsed. "No, she passed a few years back."

The practiced response sat between them like a third person. Julie nodded, filing away Carol's reaction with everything else she'd learned about reading people's true faces. The girl who'd shared summer shifts and inside jokes was now standing in Wolf's production, playing her role perfectly. She wasn't a victim. She was a partner.

A wave of nausea hit Julie—not from the revelation itself, but from how easily she'd been fooled. How many others had Carol practiced that sad smile on?

Julie smiled and raised her glass to the photo, a silent toast to whatever truth had been buried beneath this performance.

Fields had staked his spot next to 'The Farm', spinning the tale of the painting's lucky find to a captivated crowd. They hung on every word of the perfect story—too perfect, Julie recognized now.

Then up strolled a collector, a big shot known for having deep pockets. "Two grand for that Kleitsch," he said smoothly.

"Five," came a voice from the back.

"Ten."

Fields, grinning wide, raised his hands. "Let's do this properly. Live auction, right now."

Julie watched Wolf's subtle nod to Fields, the orchestrated spontaneity of it all. The bids shot up, fast and furious, until the final "Thirty-five thousand!" hung in the air and clamped down hard with "Sold!"

The room was split between clappers and those with tight smiles. 'The Farm' had gone from zero to hero in one evening, and Julie had watched the entire performance unfold like clockwork.

But she had bigger things to worry about than whether Wolf and Carol were running art scams. In her world—where her mother's murderer still walked free and she jumped at shadows—that kind of information was just another data point about who could and couldn't be trusted.

Her mother had trusted Wolf. Julie never would.

The quartet wrapped up a piece, the final note hanging in the air like a question. Julie eased her way to the exit, her heels tapping out her decision against the polished floor. She wouldn't be confronting anyone or playing detective. She'd learned the hard way that exposing liars was dangerous work, and she had bigger concerns than art fraud.

But she'd remember this night. Remember how easily a room full of smart people had been played. Remember that Wolf could orchestrate deception as smoothly as he charmed his way through social circles. Remember that Carol had chosen her side.

Julie stepped out into the cool evening air, trading the gallery's warm deception for the honest darkness of the street. In the distance, sirens wailed—a reminder that real danger was never far away, and staying alive meant picking your battles wisely.

26. THE BATTLE AFTER
THE WAR

Circles had etched into a semi-permanent residence beneath Dennis's eyes as he sank into the familiar armchair in Dr. Harris's office. The doctor closed the door and rolled his wheelchair opposite Dennis. The subdued light filtering through the curtains cast a gentle glow across the room, reflecting off the polished surfaces.

Dennis shifted uncomfortably in the seat, wringing his hands, while the clock's steady ticking punctuated the silence between them. Each tick reminded him of the metronome his mother used during his piano lessons, before the war, before everything changed.

"I'm not sleeping well," he began, his voice a hoarse whisper. His gaze drifted to a potted plant on the windowsill with its vibrant green leaves. It reminded him of the jungle outside Hue, how the green had seemed so beautiful until mortars started falling. Now, even houseplants made his chest tighten. *If plants could sense feelings, they'd wilt in my presence.*

"When I wake up at night, my head starts ruminating about this or that. Usually about the war. About Jimmy getting hit right next to me." His voice caught. "I don't get back to sleep after that. Will you prescribe sleeping pills?"

Dr. Harris leaned forward, his expression patient. "So you'd like sleeping pills to help you sleep. Are you still taking the Valium daily?"

Dennis shook his head, a slight tremor in his hands. "No, I stopped."

"Why did you stop taking the Valium?"

A weary sigh escaped Dennis, his shoulders slumping. "It makes me even more anxious. Like I'm trapped underwater, but the panic's still there."

The room fell quiet except for that relentless ticking. A torrent of thoughts crashed together. *Why can't I just be normal? Why does buying milk feel like walking through a minefield?*

"Dennis, are you with me?"

Dennis blinked, pulling himself back. "Yeah, sorry. I was..." He trailed off. How could he explain that he'd been back in that jungle clearing, watching Jimmy bleed out?

"It's all right. You stopped taking the Imipramine because of the irregular heartbeat. Have you had any panic attacks since then?"

Dennis's voice cracked. "I've had some close calls. Last Tuesday, at the hardware store when a car backfired. Yesterday, when my neighbor slammed his door. I was able to fight them off, but barely."

"How were you able to do that?"

"By getting away from whatever was triggering it. I've gotten good at running." *Does he really care, or am I just another broken veteran on his schedule?* The thought was unfair. Dr. Harris had never been anything but genuine. Still, the doubt clung to Dennis like smoke.

"We can work more on coping strategies for when anxiety is triggered. Have you tried the deep breathing exercises?"

"Yeah." Dennis's laugh was bitter. "Hard to breathe deep when you feel like you're suffocating."

"What about meditation? The TM book I recommended?"

"I got it, but..." Dennis rubbed his temples. "Sitting still with my thoughts is like being locked in a room with a rabid animal."

Dr. Harris nodded with understanding. "And the journaling?"

"Yes. I've been writing." Dennis's voice grew quieter. "About my feelings, my emotions. So far, I haven't gotten past anger and guilt. Mostly guilt." His hands clenched. "Guilty that Jimmy died and I didn't. Guilty that I'm not better at my job. Guilty that I ghosted my parents."

"Dennis, healing isn't linear. What you're experiencing..."

"Doc." Dennis looked up, meeting the psychiatrist's eyes for the first time. "I think I'm done here. I appreciate your help, but I'm getting worse instead of better. I can't work. I can't sleep. I can't even buy groceries without breaking into a sweat." His voice carried quiet finality, a surrender to the despair that had become his constant companion.

Dr. Harris was quiet for a long moment, rubbing his temple. "Most days, I sit across from men like you and hope I'm not just buying time before they break. But Dennis, this might be different. I believe it's time we consider something unconventional."

Dennis raised an eyebrow, suspicious. "Unconventional how?"

"Have you heard of psychedelic therapy?"

The question caught Dennis completely off guard. "You mean like... LSD? Doc, are you suggesting I start tripping?"

Dr. Harris smiled slightly. "It's not what you think. In controlled clinical settings, LSD has shown profound therapeutic effects for chronic anxiety and depression, particularly in veterans. This isn't about recreational drug use—it's legitimate medical treatment."

Dennis sat back, his mind reeling. *Is this real? Is my doctor actually suggesting I take acid?* "Isn't that stuff illegal?"

"For recreational use, yes. But under clinical supervision, for therapeutic purposes, it's different. There's a colleague I know—we served together in the Pacific. Let me tell you about our friend Larry."

Dr. Harris's voice took on the weight of shared experience. "Larry and I went through basic training together, fought through Okinawa, where I lost my legs. Larry came home without a scratch on the outside, but his injuries were invisible. Flashbacks, severe anxiety, nightmares. Sound familiar?"

Dennis nodded, transfixed.

"Larry tried to treat his symptoms with alcohol. Nearly killed himself. After detox at the VA, he was referred to a drug trial at Walter Reed—psychedelic therapy for addiction and trauma. They treated him with LSD under controlled conditions." Dr. Harris leaned forward. "Dennis, it didn't just cure his alcoholism. It cured his war trauma, too."

Another false hope? Another dead end? But something stirred in Dennis's chest—not quite hope, but maybe its distant cousin. "I never heard of psychedelics used in therapy."

"Only a few doctors can legally administer it. I'd like to refer you to Dr. Braunfeld. He's had remarkable success with cases like yours."

Dennis let out a brittle laugh. "Really? I took LSD once at a Grateful Dead concert. It didn't cure me—just made me paranoid about the crowd."

"That's exactly my point. Set and setting are crucial. A rock concert with thousands of strangers isn't therapeutic— it's chaotic. Dr. Braunfeld's approach is completely different."

Despite his skepticism, curiosity nudged Dennis forward. "How would it work?"

"You'll be prepared, closely monitored. Music, eye mask, a safe space. You won't be alone—not for a second. Afterward, he'll help you process and integrate the experience."

Dennis sat in the room's muted silence, 'psychedelic therapy' echoing in his mind like something from science fiction. Taking LSD was the ultimate surrender of control to the unknown. But the word 'cure' whispered seductively in his thoughts.

What if I find something inside me that's worse than the nightmares?

Then a different voice, quieter but more desperate: *I'm already living in hell. How much worse could it get?*

The war had left him with invisible shrapnel embedded in his psyche. Sleep had become an enemy, and his waking hours were a haze of hypervigilance and fatigue. His future felt like a locked door.

"Dennis," Dr. Harris's voice was gentle, "what do you think?"

Dennis closed his eyes, searching for the courage that had once carried him through jungles and firefights. When he opened them, he met Dr. Harris's gaze directly.

"What do I have to lose?" He took a shuddering breath. "Yes. I'll do it."

The words hung in the air between them, carrying the weight of all his hopes and fears. There was no turning back now. He had chosen the unknown over the unbearable familiar.

It wasn't relief. It wasn't peace. But for the first time in months, it wasn't despair.

27. OUT OF THE SYSTEM

R y's fourth cup of coffee was going cold when the phone rang. He answered without hope, already assuming it was another defrauding an innkeeper complaint. But then he heard her voice.

"It's Julie Bloom. I found out more about that loan document I showed you. About Vincent Di Nuccio."

Ray sat up straighter, hoping for a new development on the Amelia Hart case. "What did you find?"

"I'd rather show you. Can you come over?"

"Be there in twenty."

Ray parked his unmarked Ford outside Julie's house on Marine Drive. The neighborhood reminded him of Malibu— the kind of money that usually meant complications.

Julie opened the door before he could knock. She looked more worried than when he'd first seen the loan document.

"Detective, come in."

He followed her into the living room where they'd first discussed the forty-thousand-dollar loan from Vincent Di Nuccio.

She handed him a manila folder.

Ray studied the documents. Vincent Di Nuccio. Chicago Outfit. He'd heard Di Nuccio's name mentioned when he worked on an organized crime case two years ago, when he was still with the LAPD before everything went sideways.

"You just found this out?"

Julie's voice cracked. "My mother kept secrets. Good ones, apparently. I'm still finding bank accounts I didn't know existed."

Ray nodded. A hundred grand to a connected guy like Di Nuccio meant serious trouble. People who owed that kind of money to the Outfit usually ended up dead.

He stood up and shook her hand. "This confirms what we suspected. Thank you for digging deeper."

"I hope it helps you find who killed her."

As Ray slid behind the wheel, the weight of the folder in his lap told him what the records confirmed—Amelia Hart hadn't just owed money. She'd been drowning, and Di Nuccio was part of the undertow.

B ack at the station, Ray pushed aside the beach patrol reports and called his former partner at the LAPD.

"Detective Sanchez."

"Manny, it's Ray.."

"Stone? How's exile treating you?"

Ray winced. Even his friends knew what had happened. "Mostly quiet, but I have a murder case, and Vincent Di Nuccio is a person of interest. What's his current status?"

"Di Nuccio?" Manny's voice sharpened. "Still bad news. Last I heard, he was running the Stardust. Why are you poking that hornet's nest?"

"The vic owed him big money."

"Jesus. Ray, you sure you want to pursue this? After what happened with the Torrino operation..."

Ray closed his eyes. Six months later, and it still stung. One blown cover, one mistake, and his career imploded. "This is different. Can you check if he's under surveillance for any reason?"

"Give me an hour."

Ray hung up and stared at the Amelia Hart file. Maybe this case could prove he was still a real detective, not just some screwup hiding out in a beach town.

Manny called back. "The FBI likes Di Nuccio for moving stolen goods—high-end art and antiques mostly. They're handling him with kid gloves. Word is he's got protection all the way up."

"I need to interview him."

"No way. Vegas PD won't even return your calls."

Ray knew Manny was right. His blown undercover operation had made headlines. Every cop in California knew his name, and not in a good way.

R ay wrote the formal request to the Las Vegas PD anyway. He explained the financial motive and requested permission to interview Di Nuccio in person about Amelia Hart's murder. He didn't mention his history.

He mailed the request and waited, knowing it was probably hopeless.

Three days later, the response came back. Las Vegas PD would handle the interview themselves and send a transcript. Detective Stone's assistance wasn't required.

The words stung worse than he expected. They didn't just

deny his request—they denied who he used to be. Ray stared at the letter from Vegas PD. There it was in black and white:

his past still owned him.

He called Manny. "They shut me out."

"Ray, I'm sorry. Your name is still toxic. Give it time."

"Time?" Ray looked at Amelia Hart's photo and Julie's bank records. "A woman is dead because she owed money to a killer, and he thinks he's untouchable."

After hanging up, Ray sat alone in the quiet station. He'd come to Laguna Beach to rebuild his career, to prove he could still be a good cop. But maybe being a good cop sometimes meant working outside the system.

Vincent Di Nuccio thought he was safe in Vegas, protected by distance and Ray's ruined reputation.

Maybe the badge didn't open doors anymore. But it didn't stop him from kicking them down.

Ray opened Amelia Hart's file and started planning. If the system wouldn't help him get justice, he'd find another way.

28. A BEAUTIFUL LIE

W olf Schmidt adjusted his magnifying glass over a Frederic Remington catalog, making notes in the margins about brushwork techniques and color palettes. His desk was cluttered with auction records, museum catalogs, and authentication guides—all part of his methodical study of mid-nineteenth-century Western artists. The market for Remington, Catlin, and Eastman was exploding, and Wolf intended to capitalize on every detail of their styles.

The Kleitsch sale had given him the capital he needed for this new venture. Carol had played her role perfectly at the gallery opening, and the buyers had competed exactly as he'd anticipated. Now he could afford to take his time, to study the masters whose work commanded six figures at auction.

Wolf sipped his espresso as afternoon shadows stretched across his studio. The familiar thrill of a new project coursed through him—the same rush he'd felt years ago when he first realized his talent could generate serious money.

Insistent knocking interrupted his concentration. In Laguna Canyon, disruptions were inevitable—artists, hippies, and weekend tourists all wandered the winding roads. But when

Wolf opened the door, he found Julie Bloom, and her expression told him this wasn't a social call.

Wolf had always found Julie complicated. She was Amelia's daughter but closer to his age, which created an odd dynamic. While Julie had been away at college, he'd become something like family to Amelia—confidant, advisor, and eventually business partner. Now Julie stood before him with the same intelligent eyes that had always made him slightly uncomfortable.

"I need some answers," Julie said, studying his face with uncomfortable intensity.

"What's on your mind?" Wolf kept his voice casual, but something in her manner set off warning bells.

"Vincent Di Nuccio." She watched him carefully. "Tell me what that name means to you."

Wolf felt his composure slip for just a second before recovering. "Vinny? Why are you asking about him?"

"Because my mother owed him forty thousand dollars, and now she's dead." Julie's voice was steady, but her hands were clenched. "What was their relationship?"

Wolf sank into his chair, buying time. He'd known this conversation would come eventually—Julie was too smart to miss the connections forever. "Your mother had some gambling problems."

"I figured that much out. What I want to know is how Vinny fits in."

"He runs operations at the Stardust Casino. That was Amelia's favorite place to play." Wolf watched Julie's face, gauging how much she already knew.

"And when she couldn't pay her debts?"

Wolf hesitated. The truth was complicated and dangerous.

"She tried to sell him some artwork to cover what she owed."

Julie leaned forward. "What kind of artwork?"

It was the moment Wolf had dreaded. "Years ago, your mother commissioned me to create some pieces for her house. Replicas of famous paintings—Kleitsch, Wendt, some others. They were meant as decoration, conversation pieces for her parties."

"Replicas," Julie repeated slowly.

"High-quality reproductions. I'm good at what I do." Wolf spread his hands, trying to look apologetic rather than proud. "Your mother loved having beautiful things around her, even if they weren't originals."

"She tried to sell reproductions to a casino boss?"

Wolf nodded reluctantly. "She was desperate. The debts were piling up, and she thought maybe Vinny wouldn't look too closely at the provenance."

Julie gripped the back of a chair. "My God. That's fraud."

"It was a stupid risk. When she told me what she was planning, I tried to talk her out of it." Wolf's voice carried what sounded like genuine regret. "But Amelia could be stubborn when she was cornered."

"What happened when he found out?"

Wolf met Julie's eyes. "She used the house as collateral instead."

Julie was quiet for a long moment, processing. "Do you think he killed her?"

"No," Wolf said firmly. "Vinny's a businessman. Murder brings police attention, and police attention is bad for business. Besides, the loan on the house covered her debts."

"Then who?"

Wolf shook his head. "I wish I knew."

Julie stood slowly, staring at the man who'd been part of her family for years. "You were her friend, Wolf. She trusted you." Her voice carried a weight of betrayal that made Wolf look away. "If I find out you're lying to me, I won't be so polite next time."

She left without waiting for an answer, the door closing with quiet finality behind her.

Wolf poured himself a schnaps and sat in the gathering dusk of his studio. The conversation had gone better than expected—Julie suspected something, but she was asking the wrong questions.

Wolf's mind drifted back to that meeting with Vinny six months ago. The casino boss had been furious when Wolf revealed Amelia's plan to sell him forgeries, but his anger had quickly transformed into calculation when Wolf offered an alternative arrangement.

"You made these?" Vinny had asked, studying photographs of Wolf's work.

"I specialize in early California painters. Kleitsch, Wendt, Payne—I can reproduce their techniques perfectly." Vinny's thick fingers had drummed against the table.

"And you can make more?"

"As many as you want."

"We do this right—proper documentation, careful placement in auctions and private sales. We're not talking about a few quick pieces. We're talking about flooding the market systematically," Vinny said.

That conversation had changed everything. Wolf wasn't just creating the occasional forgery anymore. He was building an assembly line of deception, with Vinny's connections providing distribution and his talent providing the product.

Wolf stared into his empty glass, feeling the familiar weight of his choices. He'd started creating forgeries to pay the rent, telling himself it was temporary. But somewhere along the way, the money had become addictive, and his talent had become a prison.

Each forgery was a perfect betrayal. And Wolf Schmidt, who once painted truth for beauty's sake, now painted lies for men like Vinny Di Nuccio—and called it survival.

He poured another schnaps and returned to his Remington studies. The next masterpiece wouldn't create itself, and Vinny was expecting results.

Outside, Laguna Canyon settled into evening quiet, and Wolf continued his lonely work in the shadows between art and crime.

29. BEYOND THE SELF

D r. Gordon Braunfeld's office was in Beverly Hills, at Wilshire Boulevard and Rodeo Drive. This location screamed money Dennis didn't have.

Dennis squeezed his beat-up VW into a tight spot in the parking garage and made his way to the building. The reception area was all marble desk and abstract art—the kind of place that charged by the minute just for breathing their air.

The receptionist took his name with a professional smile and directed him to a chair near a fern that probably cost more than his monthly rent. Dennis caught himself biting his fingernails and shoved his hands in his pockets.

"Mr. Driver," the receptionist called. "Dr. Braunfeld will see you now."

Dr. Braunfeld sat behind a mahogany desk that could have doubled as a landing strip. Starched white shirt, silk tie, mustache—he looked like David Niven playing a psychiatrist.

"Hello, Dennis. Please have a seat." His voice was cultured, gentle.

Dennis settled into the teal armchair. "Well, I'm here mainly because Dr. Harris said you could cure me."

Braunfeld chuckled. "You're not the first to hope for a miracle, Dennis."

"Hope's what got me through the door, Doc."

"And it's what'll carry you through the journey. I wouldn't say 'cured,' but many people find a new perspective on their lives. That shift can be healing."

Dennis traced the armrest with his finger. "I've taken LSD once before. At a Grateful Dead concert. It didn't do much except make me paranoid."

"The context matters enormously. Set and setting—your mindset going in and the environment around you—shape the entire experience. A rock concert with thousands of strangers isn't exactly therapeutic."

Dennis's forehead creased. "I just want to sleep through the night without nightmares. Wake up without feeling like the world's about to end."

Dr. Braunfeld nodded. "Those are realistic goals. Many veterans find relief from exactly those symptoms."

"How does it work?"

"We don't fully understand the mechanism, but during those few hours, your mind can access different ways of understanding yourself and your experiences. Think of it as temporarily removing the filters that usually shape your perception."

A light knock interrupted them. A man in his thirties stepped in, casual but professional. "Ready for a little trip without moving an inch?" he asked with a grin.

Dennis looked up. "As long as it's round-trip."

"Always is. I'm Jerry."

Jerry led Dennis into a smaller room designed for comfort —soft lighting, muted blue and beige walls, thick curtains filtering sunlight into gentle patterns. A plush couch dominated the center.

"That looks more comfortable than my bed," Dennis said.

Jerry laughed. "We aim for five-star comfort. You'll be here several hours."

A pillow and blanket waited on the couch. A small table held tissues, water, and a glass. Jerry positioned his chair where he could watch without intruding.

"The music is carefully chosen to guide the experience. You won't be hungry, but you might need the bathroom. Just let me know."

Jerry offered him a small white pill and water.

Dennis's hand trembled slightly as he took the pill. "Here goes nothing. Or everything."

The tablet was bitter on his tongue before the water washed it down. He settled onto the couch, and Jerry placed a soft eye mask over his eyes. The world dimmed to comfortable darkness.

"It'll be twenty minutes or so before anything happens. Just relax and listen to the music."

The first notes were gentle, classical strings that came from everywhere at once. Dennis focused on his breathing, trying to calm the familiar flutter of anxiety in his chest. At least here, in this controlled space, he wasn't waiting for mortars to fall.

As minutes passed, something subtle shifted at the edges of his awareness. His thoughts, usually sharp and defined, began to soften around the edges. The music grew richer, more layered.

Colors began appearing behind his closed eyes—not memories or imagination, but actual visual experiences. Gentle swirls of light danced across his inner vision, growing more vivid and complex.

The room faded from his awareness. The couch beneath him became irrelevant as patterns of incredible intricacy unfolded in his mind. Geometric landscapes shifted and transformed, more beautiful than anything he'd ever seen.

Time became meaningless. The visuals intensified until Dennis felt himself merging with them, his sense of being a separate person dissolving into the flowing patterns of light and color.

The man who'd carried grief like a second spine was gone. What remained was awareness—pure, bright, boundless. He belonged to something vast and quiet and kind—the current beneath all things.

For the first time since the war, he felt no fear. No separation between himself and the world. No need to be vigilant or ready for an attack. He was connected to something that had always been there but that he'd never been able to see through the fog of trauma.

"It's okay, Dennis," Jerry's voice came from somewhere far away. "You're safe. Just let it happen."

The experience peaked in a moment of complete ego dissolution. Dennis existed as pure consciousness without boundaries, without the painful weight of his individual history.

Gradually, slowly, his sense of individual self began to reform. But something fundamental had changed. The connections he'd experienced, the love he'd felt—it was still there, accessible, real.

Jerry handed him a tissue, and Dennis realized he was crying.

. . .

ours later, Dennis sat in Dr. Braunfeld's office for a debriefing. The walls shimmered with a strange, soft brightness, and everything held traces of the journey's energy.

"I don't know how to describe it," Dennis said, his voice shaking. "I felt connected to everything. Like I was part of something infinite and loving. But the words don't come close."

"That's called ineffability," Dr. Braunfeld said gently. "The inability to adequately describe the experience in language."

"That's frustrating because I want to tell everyone. I want to shout it from the rooftops."

Dr. Braunfeld smiled with understanding. "That's a common response."

"Will this feeling last?" Dennis asked, hope naked in his voice.

"The mystical state will fade, but its effects can be permanent. Many people report lasting changes in how they see themselves and their place in the world."

Dennis nodded slowly. "I had insights that felt incredibly important. Like I understood things about life and death and meaning that I'd never grasped before. Were they real?"

"Your mind experienced what it's like when the sense of being a separate, isolated self dissolves. Whether that's 'real' depends on how you define reality. But yes, I believe it changes who you are going forward."

They sat quietly for a moment. Dennis wasn't the same man who had walked in that morning. The war was still part of his history, but it no longer felt like his entire identity.

For the first time in years, he wasn't afraid of going to sleep.

30. THE INTERVIEW

Ray's hands shook slightly as he packed his briefcase. Manny had pulled strings with Vegas PD, and Ray finally had his shot at Vincent Di Nuccio.

He'd barely slept, his mind cycling through questions and strategies. This was his chance to prove he was still a real detective, not just some screwup hiding out in a beach town.

The flight to Vegas was turbulence and stale coffee. Ray stared out the window, rehearsing the interview in his head. Di Nuccio would be smooth, prepared, and probably lawyered up. But Ray had spent years reading liars—his reputation might be shot, but his instincts were still sharp.

McCarran Airport hit him like a wall of cigarette smoke and slot machine bells. Even the terminal was gambling-obsessed, with tourists feeding quarters into machines while waiting for flights.

Detective Pierce, his chaperone from Las Vegas PD, met him at baggage claim—a thick-set guy in a plaid sports jacket who looked like he'd rather be anywhere else.

"You're the Laguna Beach cop?" Pierce asked, lighting a cigarette before they'd even left the terminal.

"That's me."

They got into Pierce's unmarked car, which smelled like an ashtray. Ray rolled down his window.

"So what's Di Nuccio's deal?" Ray asked as they drove through the desert heat toward the Strip.

"He runs the Stardust for the Chicago mob." Pierce flicked ash out his window. "Why's a small-town detective interested in him?"

"Dead woman owed him money, a lot ot of money."

Pierce snorted. "Doesn't surprise me. Vinny's got a thing for ladies with gambling problems. Builds relationships, if you know what I mean."

Ray watched the neon signs blur past. "What kind of relationships?"

"The profitable kind. He runs an art gallery in the casino, plus a high-end antique shop downtown. Perfect setup for moving money around."

The Stardust's sign blazed like a neon promise—glory for the lucky, ruin for the rest. Ray felt his chest tighten with the familiar focus that came before a big interview.

Inside, the casino was all flashing lights and the constant ding of slot machines. Pierce led him through the maze of gaming tables toward the back offices, past security guards who watched everything with dead eyes.

"Remember," Pierce said as they walked, "This is my jurisdiction. Let me introduce you, then you can take the lead."

Vincent Di Nuccio's office was designed to impress—mahogany desk, leather chairs, expensive art on the walls. The man himself was smaller than Ray had expected, with carefully styled silver hair and a bespoke suit.

"Gentlemen, please sit." Di Nuccio's voice was smooth, cultured. "I understand you're here about poor Amelia."

Ray settled into the chair across from the desk. "You knew Mrs. Hart well?"

"Amelia was a valued guest of the Stardust. Her death was a shock—such a vibrant woman." Di Nuccio's mouth smiled, but his eyes stayed still. Calculating. Waiting.

"She gambled here regularly?"

"She enjoyed the finer things. We provided a suite, transportation, and VIP treatment. Amelia appreciated quality."

Ray leaned forward slightly. "She got in over her head?"

Di Nuccio shrugged. "It happens. The house always wins eventually."

"You lent her money?"

"I provided financial assistance against her estate. A gentleman's agreement between friends."

"Friends?" Ray kept his voice neutral. "Is that standard practice for your big losers?"

"Amelia wasn't just another gambler. We had business discussions—she was interested in opening an art gallery. Something classy for high-end clients."

Ray made a note. Art again. Everything in this case came back to art. "You visited her in Laguna Beach?"

"New Year's Eve. She was proud of her home, wanted to show it off. Beautiful place, incredible art collection."

"What time did you leave that night?"

"Just before midnight. I wanted to call my wife and wish her Happy New Year at midnight."

Ray studied Di Nuccio's face. The man's fingers drummed once against his desk, then stopped. "You flew back that night?"

"Company jet. From Long Beach," Di Nuccio said quickly, a

fraction too fast. It sounded rehearsed—like a detail he'd been waiting to deliver.

"Anyone else travel with you?"

"Just the pilot and co-pilot."

Pierce had been silent throughout the interview, occasionally taking notes. Now he spoke up. "We may need to verify your flight records."

"Of course. My assistant can provide whatever you need."

Ray stood up. "Thank you for your time, Mr. Di Nuccio."

"I hope you find whoever did this terrible thing. Amelia deserved better."

Outside the casino, Pierce lit another cigarette. "What do you think?"

"He's lying about something," Ray said. "But I'm not sure what."

"The flight story seemed solid."

Ray shook his head. "Too solid. Like he'd rehearsed it."

They drove back to the airport in relative silence. Ray's mind was working through the interview, cataloging details and inconsistencies. Di Nuccio had been smooth, prepared—but there were cracks in his story.

On the plane back to Orange County, Ray stared out at the desert passing below. The interview had revealed more questions than answers, but that was often how these cases worked.

Di Nuccio's story held together too neatly. The gallery, the VIP treatment, the midnight to his wife—every detail polished to gleam. And that gleam felt like camouflage.

Ray pulled out his notebook and started writing down everything he could remember from the interview. If Di

Nuccio thought one interview would end this investigation, he was wrong.

Amelia Hart deserved justice, and Ray Stone was going to make sure she got it.

The plane hit turbulence as they descended toward Orange County, jolting Ray from his thoughts. Control was an illusion —Amelia had learned that the hard way. But some things you could control, like not giving up when the case got complicated.

Ray looked out at the lights of Orange County below and felt something he hadn't experienced in months: purpose. He was back in the game, and this time he wasn't going to blow it.

31. THE WEIGHT WE CARRY

Dennis walked the morning streets of Laguna Beach at a pace that would have frustrated him a week ago. Before Dr. Braunfeld's treatment, he'd moved through town like a man late for his own funeral—head down, shoulders tight, always checking over his shoulder for threats that existed only in his hypervigilant mind.

Now he noticed things. The way morning light filtered through the marine layer. The sound of his footsteps on uneven pavement. The fact that he wasn't constantly scanning for danger.

He spotted Bob shuffling toward him with that enormous backpack, same as always. For months, Dennis had given the homeless man nothing more than a quick nod—acknowledgment without engagement, the bare minimum of human decency. Today felt different.

"Morning, Bob," Dennis said, actually stopping instead of hurrying past. "That pack looks heavy."

Bob's weathered face split into a grin. "This old thing? It's my whole world right here. I'm what you might call an urban naturalist."

Dennis laughed—a real laugh, not the bitter chuckle that had been his default for years. "Urban naturalist? What's that involve?"

"Finding nature everywhere, even in the city. You'd be surprised what grows in the cracks of sidewalks, what birds make homes in traffic lights." Bob shifted the pack on his shoulders. "Most people walk right past it all."

Dennis had been one of those people. "Like what?"

"See that weed there?" Bob pointed to a scraggly plant pushing through a crack in the concrete. "Ice plant. Tough little survivor. Been growing in that same spot for two years, and the city keeps trying to kill it with weed killer. But it keeps coming back."

Something about that resonated with Dennis. "Persistent."

"That's the thing about life—it finds a way. Even when everything's stacked against it." Bob's eyes crinkled. "Kind of like people, don't you think?"

Dennis studied the plant, really looked at it. That plant had been there all along. He'd just never had the eyes to see it.

"Most folks don't notice," Bob continued. "They're too busy getting where they're going to see where they are."

The words hit Dennis like a gentle slap. How many years had he spent getting somewhere else instead of being present?

"You carrying everything you own in there?" Dennis asked, gesturing to the backpack.

"Pretty much. But I like to think of it as traveling light. No mortgage, no car payments, no stuff I don't need." Bob grinned. "Freedom's got its own weight to it."

Dennis had spent years feeling trapped by his own mind, his own memories. The idea of that kind of freedom seemed both terrifying and appealing. "Doesn't it get lonely?"

"Sometimes. But you meet interesting people when you're

paying attention. Like right now—we've been neighbors for months, and this is the first real conversation we've had."

Dennis felt heat in his cheeks. Bob was right. "I haven't been much of a neighbor, have I?"

"You've been dealing with your own stuff. We all are." Bob adjusted his pack straps. "The thing about being out here is you learn to see people for who they are right now, not who they used to be or who they might become."

That hit Dennis hard. He'd been so defined by what had happened to him in Vietnam, by his failures and fears, that he'd forgotten he was more than his trauma.

"Listen, Bob, if you want to leave your pack at my place during the day, you're welcome. I live just up the hill. Might be easier to explore without carrying your whole world around."

Bob studied him for a moment, as if looking for the catch. "You serious?"

"Yeah. I work from home, so someone's usually there. And honestly..." Dennis paused, surprised by his own honesty. "I could use the company."

"Groovy," Bob said, and his relief was obvious. "That's really decent of you, man."

Dennis scribbled his address on a scrap of paper. Such a small gesture, but it felt significant—like opening a door he'd kept locked for years.

Something opened in his chest. Space. Room for another person. Room for grace.

"Thanks, Dennis. Really." Bob tucked the paper into his shirt pocket. "See you around."

. . .

Later, Dennis sat on a bench at Monument Point, watching waves crash against the rocks. Just a few days ago, the sound might have reminded him of distant artillery fire.. Now it was just water meeting stone, nothing more, nothing less.

He thought of the swirling lights from his session with Dr. Braunfeld, how they'd pulsed like breath. Now the waves felt the same—slow, steady, and alive.

The conversation with Bob had stirred something in him. For years, he'd measured his worth by external achievements, but what had any of that mattered when his mind was trapped in a war that was over for him?

He thought about Bob's backpack, containing everything the man owned but somehow representing freedom rather than a burden. Dennis had filled his life with possessions and obligations, thinking they would make him secure. Instead, they'd become a different kind of weight.

A pelican landed on the rocks, unafraid, just going about its business. Dennis saw the bird not as a symbol, but as kin. Just another survivor, navigating the world without apology. The sun warmed his face, and for the first time in years, Dennis wasn't planning his next move or ruminating over old regrets. He was just sitting by the ocean, feeling grateful for a conversation with a man he'd ignored for months.

Maybe this was what healing looked like—not the absence of problems, but the presence of connection. Not forgetting the past, but not being imprisoned by it either.

Dennis closed his eyes and listened to the endless conversation between water and shore.

32. GHOSTS AND SUSPECTS

Detective Ray Stone sat behind a stack of case files when Nadine called over the partition. "Dennis Driver's here to see you."

Dennis walked in looking different—relaxed in a way Ray hadn't seen before. He took the chair across from Ray's desk without his usual fidgeting.

"So what happened with that CIA art theft theory?" Ray asked, leaning back in his chair.

Dennis smiled, actually smiled. "Turns out it was just a regular burglary. No international conspiracy."

"Just a small-time thief with two burglary priors. Nothing professional. But he's ready to talk," Ray said. "He wants to make a deal with the DA."

Dennis nodded, seemingly distracted by the dying plant on top of Ray's filing cabinet. "This little guy needs water."

Ray raised an eyebrow. "My conspiracy theorist has become a gardener?"

"Something like that." Dennis looked out the window at the street below. "About that whole thing, Ray... I owe you an apology."

Ray waited, sensing Dennis needed to get this out.

"I was seeing patterns that weren't there. The CIA, communist plots—I was chasing ghosts." Dennis met Ray's eyes. "I was pretty messed up in the head."

"We all have bad cases," Ray said. "The trick is knowing when to step back."

"You helped me with the sketch artist, took me seriously when I probably sounded crazy. You didn't have to do that."

Ray shrugged. "You had good instincts, just needed better direction. Sharp minds can cut both ways."

Dennis stood up. "I owe you one. When you need something, just ask."

As Dennis left, Ray felt a rare warmth—respect not just for the apology, but for the man who'd found a way back from the edge.

T he next morning, Ray called Detective Pat Ahern at the county jail.

Our boy's talking," Ahern said. "Says he was hired by someone called 'Jack.' No last name, but claims the guy's big in the John Birch Society. Real paranoid about communists."

Ray sat up straighter. "Interesting. I've got a 'Jack' I like for the Hart murder."

"Got a photo? Our thief will identify him for a sentence reduction."

"I'll get one," Ray said. "Talk soon."

Ray hung up and thought about Jack Hart. The man had every reason to hate Amelia—politically, personally, ideologically. All that rage, just waiting for an excuse. Jack's bitterness about his father marrying Amelia after divorcing his mother. His political paranoia, his obsession with communist threats.

And Amelia's final painting, with its anti-war message, would have been the perfect trigger. Everything pointed to Jack Hart. Ray just needed proof.

R ay drove to Corona del Mar and parked across from Jack Hart's office building. He'd called earlier to confirm Hart was in. Now he waited, camera ready, newspaper spread across the steering wheel as cover.

The 35mm camera sat beside him, telephoto lens attached. The midday glare off the office windows made it hard to see inside, but Ray was patient. He'd done plenty of surveillance in his LAPD days.

The Ford's interior heated up despite the open windows. Ray shifted occasionally, wiping sweat from his forehead. The air smelled like exhaust and ocean salt.

Dennis had described Jack Hart perfectly—receding hairline, average height, the look of a man carrying grudges. Ray studied everyone who passed, waiting for the right face.

Lunch hour brought foot traffic. Business suits mixed with casual beach wear. Seagulls fought over scraps near the restaurant patios. The smell of grilled onions drifted from nearby eateries.

Ray's fingers tapped out a rhythm of focus—slow, steady, waiting. He'd been at this for two hours, but patience was part of the job. Good surveillance couldn't be rushed.

Then the office door opened, and Jack Hart stepped out.

"There we go," Ray muttered, raising the camera.

Hart paused on the sidewalk, checking his watch. Ray clicked off several shots. Hart turned, giving Ray a perfect profile view. More clicks.

Hart paused, glanced once toward the street. Ray didn't

flinch. Just another man behind a newspaper, watching the world go by.

Hart walked toward his car, unaware he was being documented. Ray caught him from multiple angles as he moved down the street. Each shot was potential evidence, a piece of the puzzle that would connect Jack Hart to Amelia's murder.

Ray lowered the camera, satisfied. He had what he needed for Detective Ahern. If the burglar identified Hart, they'd have their first real break in the case.

Ray started the Ford and pulled into traffic. After months of dead ends and jurisdictional roadblocks, the investigation was finally moving forward. Jack Hart might think he'd gotten away with murder, but Ray Stone was patient, methodical, and very good at his job.

The hunt was closing in.

33. WHAT WE DON'T SAY

Dennis walked through the Hart property gate, salt air mixing with the scent of jasmine from the garden. He paused, realizing he hadn't checked over his shoulder once—a small miracle he barely noticed. The hypervigilance that had ruled his life for years had finally loosened its grip.

Julie opened the door with a smile, "Come in. I was just looking at Mom's paintings."

Inside the great room, Dennis stood before Amelia's artwork on the north wall. The chaotic brushstrokes and violent imagery no longer triggered his own war memories—now he could appreciate the artist's attempt to capture trauma in paint. He understood that impulse.

"She was trying to say something important," he said, studying the anti-war piece. "Even if people didn't want to hear it."

Julie settled into one of the armchairs. "Speaking of that painting—the police caught the thief who took 'Body Count.'"

"Really? Anyone you know?

"Career burglar, apparently. But someone paid him to steal

it." Dennis took the chair across from her. "Looks like some right-wing group didn't appreciate your mother's message."

Julie's laugh was bitter. "All that drama over a painting. William Fields said nobody wanted to buy anyway."

They sat in comfortable silence for a moment, the golden afternoon light shifting across the room. Dennis found himself noticing details he would have missed months ago— the way dust motes danced in the sunbeams, the distant sound of waves against the cliffs.

"Want to get some air?" he asked.

Outside, they walked toward the bluff overlooking the ocean. When Dennis brushed a leaf from Julie's hair, he was surprised by how natural the gesture felt. A month ago, an unexpected touch would have made him flinch. Now his hands were steady, gentle.

"There's a fire down there," Julie said, pointing to the beach below, where smoke drifted up from a small campfire.

A metal staircase zigzagged down the cliff face to a secluded beach. A group of teenagers had gathered around the fire, and their boat was pulled up on the sand.

"Do you know them?" Dennis asked.

"Local kids. They've been coming here for years, much to Mom's annoyance. Nothing she could do about it, though. The beach is public property up to the high tide mark..." Julie's expression darkened slightly. "I'm going to miss this place,"

Dennis placed his hand on her shoulder.

"You know what's weird?" Julie looked at him. "I lived with Mom for eighteen years, and I barely knew her. How does that happen?"

Dennis thought about his own family, the things he'd never told them about the war, the distance he'd created to protect them from his pain. "Maybe that's what growing up really is.

Learning that our parents are just people, trying to figure it out like the rest of us."

Julie was quiet for a moment. "I was away at school for four years and didn't come home much. When I did, it was all about me—my problems, my plans. I never asked about her life."

"That doesn't make you a bad daughter."

"Doesn't it?" Julie's voice cracked slightly. "I grew closer to my dad during those same years. He was in LA and made himself available when I needed him. But Mom..." She shrugged helplessly.

Dennis could hear the pain in her voice. Six months ago, he couldn't have handled someone else's emotions. His own were too overwhelming. Now he found himself wanting to help carry her burden.

"Dennis, can I tell you something? Something I've never told anyone except my dad?"

He nodded, sensing the weight of what was coming.

"When I was a junior at UCLA, I fell in love with this guy. Really fell. Completely lost myself in it." Julie's hands trembled as she clasped them together. "When he dumped me, I couldn't handle it. I stopped going to classes, barely left my room."

Dennis waited, letting her set the pace.

"Then I found out I was pregnant." Her voice dropped to a whisper. "I thought about killing myself."

The words hit Dennis like a physical blow, not because they triggered his own darkness, but because he could feel her pain so clearly. "Jesus, Julie."

"I never told Mom. How can I be angry with her for keeping secrets when I did the same thing?" Tears started streaming down her face. "I kept her locked out of the most important thing that ever happened to me."

When Dennis saw her tears, something clenched in his chest, not anxiety or panic, but pure compassion; he moved closer, putting his arm around her shoulders. "What happened?"

"I finally called Dad. He took me home with him." Julie leaned into Dennis's embrace. "He helped me get counseling, supported me through the abortion. Never judged me, just loved me back to sanity."

Dennis felt the profound trust she was showing him. "Your mom never knew?"

"Never. I took a semester off, got help, and came back stronger. But I shut her out of all of it." Julie looked up at him. "I know something about keeping secrets. About thinking you're protecting people by not telling them how bad things really were."

Their eyes met, and Dennis saw his own understanding reflected there. "Sometimes the secrets hurt more than the truth would have."

"Yes," Julie said simply.

They stood there as the first stars appeared, holding each other against the gathering darkness. Dennis marveled at the change in himself. Six months ago, he couldn't handle his own emotions, let alone help someone else with theirs. Dr. Braunfeld's treatment hadn't just healed his trauma; it had given him the capacity to really be present for another person.

Julie looked up at him, her face soft in the starlight. Then something shifted in her expression—uncertainty, maybe fear of having revealed too much. She started to pull back slightly.

Dennis felt the moment balanced on a knife's edge. He could let her retreat, protect herself behind familiar walls. Instead, he gently cupped her face in his hands, anchoring them both in the present moment.

"Thank you for trusting me with that," he said quietly.

The uncertainty in her eyes melted into something deeper. When she pressed her lips to his, it felt like a question and an answer at the same time. Dennis kissed her back, tasting salt from her tears and something deeper—trust, vulnerability, hope.

When they broke apart, he rested his forehead against hers. "Thank you for being someone I could trust," she whispered.

Dennis held her close as the teenagers' laughter drifted up from the beach below. He knew this moment was fragile—Julie would be leaving soon, Jack Hart was pushing for a quick sale, and his own healing was still being tested daily. But for now, holding her as the ocean whispered against the cliffs, it was enough.

More than enough. It was everything he'd never thought he'd be capable of having.

34. ALMOST TOO GOOD TO
BE TRUE

The Butterfield Auction House exhaled history and money in equal measure, the air thick with the scent of wax polish and old canvas. Wolf positioned himself near the valuation counter, close enough to observe Carol but far enough to avoid the security cameras he'd mapped during previous visits. The soft murmur of appraised values drifted through the room like a constant prayer to commerce.

Carol stood in line clutching a Robinson's Department Store shopping bag, two framed paintings hidden inside. Her posture was perfect—nervous enough to seem authentic, composed enough to inspire confidence. Wolf had coached her for hours, but watching her now, he felt an unexpected tightness in his chest. She trusted him completely, believed they were partners in this grand adventure. She had no idea how expendable that made her.

Wolf scanned the room. The security guard by the entrance, the cameras in the corners, the flow of foot traffic—all catalogued and assessed. Since Amelia's death, he'd noticed increased police activity around the art scene. Detective Stone had been asking questions, and Julie was growing more suspicious. Maybe it was time to be more careful.

The man ahead of Carol wore a cowboy hat and clutched what looked like a landscape. He shuffled away from the counter with hunched shoulders. Another hopeful seller was disappointed. The screener, a sharp-eyed woman in her thirties, gestured Carol forward.

Carol placed her paintings on the counter with steady hands, though Wolf caught the slight tremor in her fingers as she adjusted the frames. "I'd like these evaluated for auction, please."

The screener's eyes brightened as she examined the pieces. She lifted the Remington first, angling it toward the light. Wolf's jaw tightened as she lingered over one corner of the canvas on the exact spot where he'd aged the paint with coffee grounds and cigarette ash.

"Can you tell me how you acquired these?" the screener asked.

"I inherited them from my grandfather's estate," Carol replied, her voice steadier than Wolf had expected. "My mother thinks they might be valuable."

"I'll get our American art expert. Please wait here."

Wolf turned away and wandered into the adjacent viewing room, maintaining his cover. He'd spent too many hours in these halls lately—someone sharp might start to notice patterns. But the education was invaluable, and the money was too good to stop.

A man in a double-knit suit approached Carol, adjusting his wire-rimmed glasses with the obsessive precision of someone who'd spent decades staring at brushstrokes. Wolf positioned himself behind a display cabinet, close enough to observe but ready to disappear if needed.

The expert examined the Eastman first, clicking his tongue softly, a habit that suggested years of making these judgments. "Nice little Seth Eastman. Maybe fifteen hundred to two thousand, depending on the market's mood." Wolf's pulse quickened. So far, so good.

The expert turned to the Remington, and Wolf held his breath. This was the more ambitious forgery, the one that could either make them rich or expose them completely. "My, my, this Remington has been beautifully restored," His voice carried genuine admiration as he clicked his tongue again. "Superb work. Do you know who handled the restoration?"

Wolf couldn't suppress a slight smile. The man was praising restoration work that had never happened—every crack, every faded brushstroke was Wolf's deliberate creation.

"No, I inherited it as is," Carol replied.

"Remarkable craftsmanship. Do you have others like these in the estate?"

Carol glanced toward Wolf's general direction, a movement so brief only he would notice. "Yes, several more."

"I'd be very interested in seeing them. Very interested indeed." The expert's eyes gleamed behind his glasses. "How much are you hoping to get for the Remington?"

"I'm not sure what it's worth."

"At least twenty-five hundred, possibly more. The conservation work alone saves a buyer considerable expense." The expert gestured to his assistant. "Please prepare formal valuations for both pieces."

Outside in the Los Angeles afternoon, Wolf felt the excruciating mixture of exhilaration and unease that followed every successful con.

"Did you see his face when he looked at the Remington?" Carol asked, her eyes bright with excitement. "That little tongue-clicking thing he did, like he'd found buried treasure."

"He was practically drooling," Wolf replied, but something nagged at him. The expert had been almost too interested, too eager to see more pieces.

"Your work is incredible," Carol said, reaching for his hand. "The way you aged that canvas. He actually complimented your restoration work."

Wolf nodded, watching her fingers intertwine with his. She squeezed his hand, and he felt that familiar hollow sensation— the recognition that she loved an illusion, believed in a partnership that existed only in her imagination. For a moment, he wondered what it would be like to deserve that trust.

"That was almost too easy," Carol continued.

"That's what worries me," Wolf said, pushing down the unexpected guilt. "When something seems too easy, it usually means you're missing something."

Carol's smile faltered slightly. "You think he suspected?"

"No, but he's very interested. Maybe too interested." Wolf glanced back at the auction house. "We need to be careful about how many pieces we feed through Butterfield's. Success breeds attention."

"Are you worried about the police investigation?"

Wolf had been trying not to think about Detective Stone's persistence or Julie's growing suspicions. "I'm worried about getting sloppy. The more successful we become, the more visible we are."

Carol linked her arm through his, trusting and warm against his side. "We make a good team."

Wolf smiled, though they both understood the reality. He was the talent: she was the face. Useful, attractive, convincing, and ultimately replaceable. The thought should have felt empowering, but instead, it left him strangely empty. "The world is full of possibilities for people like us," he said instead.

As they walked toward his car, Wolf caught a glimpse of a black sedan parked across the street. Nothing unusual about that, except he was almost certain he'd seen the same car near his studio twice this week.

He didn't mention it to Carol. No point in making her nervous over what was probably nothing.

But Wolf Schmidt had survived this long by trusting his instincts, and right now, his instincts were telling him that their charmed run might be coming to an end. The question was whether he'd have the courage to protect Carol when it did, or if his survival instincts would prove stronger than whatever remained of his conscience.

35. PATRIOTS AND PRETENDERS

Dennis's phone rang at 6 AM, cutting through the pre-dawn quiet like a blade and jolting him from the uneasy sleep that had plagued him since the bluff. His dreams had been filled with fragments—Julie's tears, the crashing waves below, shadows moving through the darkness. The harsh ring seemed to echo in his cramped apartment, bouncing off the sparse furnishings that marked his new civilian life.

Ray's voice crackled through the receiver, tight with the kind of frustration Dennis recognized from his military days—the sound of a man under pressure with time running out. "I'm looking into the connection between the John Birch Society connection to Jack Hart and Amelia Hart's murder. What can you tell me about the Brichers?"

Dennis sat up in bed. His mind cleared immediately, shifting from the fog of sleep to sharp focus. The morning light filtering through his thin curtains cast long shadows across the room, and he could hear the distant hum of early commuter traffic beginning to build on the Coast Highway.

"I might be able to help with that," Dennis said, his voice steady despite the adrenaline now coursing through his system. "There's this guy at work—Martin. He's a Bircher, no question about it. Always trying to recruit me, dropping hints about the communist threat, wearing that JBS pin like a badge of honor."

"Good. See what you can find out what he knows about Jack Hart."

"Will do."

The Daily Pilot newsroom buzzed with its usual morning energy—typewriters clacking, phones ringing, the sharp scent of cigarette smoke mixing with fresh coffee. Dennis made his way through the maze of desks, nodding to colleagues while scanning for Martin's familiar profile. He found him hunched over a stack of papers near the sports desk. Martin looked up as Dennis approached, his thin face brightening with the eager expression of a man always ready to convert the unconvinced.

Dennis pulled up a chair, keeping his voice casual despite the urgency thrumming beneath his skin. "You mentioned some influential people in the organization. Ever heard of Jack Hart?"

Martin's eyes lit up like Christmas morning. He leaned forward, lowering his voice to a conspiratorial whisper that made Dennis's skin crawl.

"Everyone knows Jack. Sharp businessman, real patriot. Understands what this country's up against better than most." Martin's fingers drummed against his desk with nervous energy. "Why do you ask?"

"Read something about his oil company. Seems like the kind of man who gets things done."

"Oh, he does. Jack doesn't just talk about fighting the communist infiltration; he acts. Been with JBS for years, really stepped up his involvement lately." Martin's voice carried the reverence of a true believer. "Matter of fact, he'll be at the meeting tonight. Why don't you come and check it out?"

Dennis felt his pulse quicken. The pieces were falling into place faster than he'd hoped, but he kept his expression neutral, mildly interested rather than hungry for information.

"Meeting?"

"Monthly gathering. Nothing fancy, just concerned citizens discussing the threats facing our nation. Jack usually speaks. He has a brilliant mind for strategy. You'd learn a lot."

The typewriter keys seemed louder now, each strike echoing in Dennis's ears as he weighed his options. This could be exactly what Ray needed—a direct connection between Jack Hart and the organization that had been threatening Amelia. But walking into a room full of John Birch Society members felt like stepping into enemy territory.

"Where and when?"

Martin scribbled an address on a piece of paper, his handwriting precise and careful. "Seven o'clock. Newport Beach Community Center. Ask for the Patriots' Room."

Dennis pocketed the paper, already planning his approach. "Thanks, Martin. Sounds interesting."

As Martin walked away, Dennis realized what he was committing to. He was planning to infiltrate a group of potential extremists with less than twelve hours to prepare. The distinction between courage and recklessness seemed increasingly unclear—especially when someone else might pay the price for his choices.

. . .

The Community Center smelled of coffee and nervous sweat, the close air thick with the tension of true believers. A malfunctioning fluorescent light flickered overhead, casting intermittent shadows that made Dennis's eyes water. He positioned himself three rows from the back, close enough to hear clearly but far enough to avoid notice. He'd chosen a seat near the side exit.

Dennis poured himself coffee from the urn in the corner and immediately regretted it—bitter coffee that tasted like it had been sitting for hours. He forced himself to sip it anyway, needing something to occupy his hands while he scanned the room, cataloging faces and exits. His heart rate remained steady despite the circumstances. Dr. Braunfeld's treatment had taught him that emotions were temporary visitors, not permanent residents. This anxiety would pass.

Then he saw Jack Hart across the room, and his stomach dropped.

Hart was working the crowd like a politician with an election coming up, but his movements had the confidence of someone in his element. This wasn't just attendance, but leadership.

"Jack! Over here!" called a robust voice from the corner.

Hart navigated through the crowd, backslapping as he went. "Tom, you old hawk. How's the family?"

"Better for seeing you, Jack. Kids are growing like weeds."

A business-suited woman approached, and Dennis caught the deference in her posture. "What about you, Jack? Still fighting the good fight?"

Hart's laugh was low and confident. "Someone's got to

stand up for traditional values, Diane. Especially after our recent success." He glanced around the room with satisfaction. "Sometimes problems solve themselves when patriots pay attention."

Dennis leaned forward, straining to catch Hart's next words.

"Take that Hart woman—no relation, thank God. All that anti-war poison she was spreading to impressionable young minds. Well, let's just say some voices don't need to be heard anymore."

The woman at the podium cleared her throat, calling for attention. "This month, our educational films reached three more schools. Young people need to understand the threats facing our country. We can't let communist sympathizers corrupt another generation."

Murmurs of approval rustled through the crowd. Dennis leaned toward the matronly woman beside him. "Important work."

She beamed. "Oh yes, awareness is key. We discussed the Laguna Artist situation at my bridge club just last week." Her voice dropped to a conspiratorial whisper. "Amazing how quickly certain voices can be silenced when real patriots take coordinated action."

"She thought she was untouchable," someone behind Dennis said quietly. "Well, we showed her what happens to traitors."

Another voice, barely audible: "New Year's Eve was quite the celebration, wasn't it? One less communist sympathizer poisoning young minds."

Dennis's blood ran cold. They weren't just talking about silencing opposition. They were celebrating Amelia's murder.

He forced himself to join the scattered applause with hollow claps, watching Hart accept quiet congratulations from several attendees.

As the formal meeting wound down, Dennis remained seated, waiting for the crowd to thin. Jack Hart was still there, holding court with his inner circle, accepting praise like a war hero. Dennis needed to get closer, to hear what they said when they thought only allies were listening.

But as he stood to move, Hart's eyes found his across the room. Recognition dawned slowly on Hart's face, followed by something much more dangerous. Hart excused himself from his group and walked directly toward Dennis, his expression shifting from confusion to cold calculation.

"Well, well. Dennis Driver from the Daily Pilot." Hart's voice was friendly, but his eyes were ice. "Funny seeing you here. You following me?"

"Just trying to understand different perspectives," Dennis said, his voice steadier than he felt.

Hart studied him for a long moment, then smiled. "You know, Dennis, I've been reading your articles about poor Amelia. Very... thorough reporting."

The way Hart said "thorough" made Dennis's skin crawl.

"Fact is," Hart continued, stepping closer and lowering his voice to a whisper only Dennis could hear, "I know quite a bit about you. Your service record. Your breakdown. Your treatment with Dr. Braunfeld." Hart's smile widened. "Funny thing about reporters with Vietnam Syndrome. They have episodes. Breakdowns. Sometimes they hurt people they care about."

The threat hit Dennis like a physical blow. Hart had done his homework—he knew about the treatment, probably knew about Julie too.

"Be a real shame if Julie Bloom had to deal with another

tragedy so soon after losing her mother," Hart continued, his voice still conversational. "Mental health is so fragile, isn't it? Especially in veterans. Sometimes they just... snap."

Dennis felt the room spinning slightly, but forced himself to maintain eye contact. "Good evening, Mr. Hart."

Hart's hand clamped down on Dennis's shoulder, fingers digging in just hard enough to hurt. "Oh, I'm sure we'll be seeing more of each other very soon. In fact, I'd bet on it. And Dennis?" Hart's grip tightened. "Be careful driving home tonight. These roads can be dangerous for people who aren't paying attention."

Dennis turned and walked toward the exit, feeling Hart's gaze burning into his back. The door seemed miles away, but he forced himself to maintain a steady pace. *Don't run. Don't give him the satisfaction. Don't let him see how rattled you are.*

He reached the door and stepped into the cool night air, his lungs filling with relief. But as he walked toward his car, Dennis noticed Hart at the church window, watching Dennis's every move. Two men Dennis recognized from the meeting were already in the parking lot, moving toward separate vehicles.

Dennis started his engine, heart hammering. In his rearview mirror, he saw one of the men getting into a dark sedan while the other climbed into a pickup truck. They followed him down the Coast Highway. When Dennis turned right toward Julie's house, both vehicles followed.

Dennis took a circuitous route through residential neighborhoods, watching both vehicles match his every turn. Hart's threats echoed in his mind: *Sometimes they just snap.* The bastard was planning to make Dennis look like he'd had a breakdown, hurt Julie, maybe killed himself. The perfect way to discredit any evidence Dennis might have gathered.

Finally, Dennis pulled into the Von's Market parking lot and waited. The sedan drove past without slowing, but the pickup truck parked across the street with a clear view of Dennis's position. They weren't trying to hide anymore—they wanted him to know he was being watched.

36. PAINTED INTO A CORNER

Wolf gripped the steering wheel of his new Ford van as he and Carol drove through the desert darkness toward Las Vegas. He'd purchased the vehicle with some of the loot from the forged Kleitsch painting, "The Farm". Each mile brought them closer to a business relationship with Vinny Di Nuccio, the man who had probably murdered Amelia Ha

Vinny's words from their last phone call echoed in his mind: "Dead women tell no tales." Had that been a general observation about the benefits of Amelia's death, or something closer to a confession?

"You're quiet tonight," Carol observed, adjusting the radio as neon signs began appearing in the distance.

Wolf forced a smile. "Can't stop thinking about business."

But what he was really thinking about was how Amelia had ended up at the bottom of that cliff on New Year's Eve, and whether the man they were about to meet had pushed her there over forty thousand dollars in gambling debts.

. . .

The Stardust Hotel blazed against the night sky like a monument to greed and excess. As they pulled into the parking lot, Wolf felt his stomach clench. Every successful forgery had bound him tighter to Vinny's criminal operation, made him more complicit in whatever had happened to Amelia.

In the lobby, slot machines chirped and jangled while fortune-seekers fed them coins with mechanical devotion. Wolf approached the check-in counter, their oversized suitcase heavy in his hand—not just with clothes, but with two carefully crafted forgeries that would either make them rich or get them killed.

"Mr. and Mrs. Schmidt, your suite awaits," the desk clerk announced with practiced enthusiasm.

Their room was a shrine to expensive taste—red shag carpet, gold brocade drapes, and a crystal decanter that filled the air with the scent of luxury. It was the kind of place that whispered of power and violence in equal measure.

"I feel like a five-hundred-dollar hooker in this place," Carol laughed, spinning in her dress.

Wolf's smile felt sick. The luxury was Vinny's way of showing his power. He could give them anything, which meant he could take everything away just as easily, including their lives, if Wolf's suspicions about Amelia were correct.

A knock at the door made Wolf's pulse spike. He opened it to reveal Vinny Di Nuccio's silhouette framed by the hallway's golden glow.

Vinny entered the room like he owned it, which he did. But Wolf couldn't shake the image of this same man visiting Amelia's house on New Year's Eve, perhaps discussing her gambling debts one final time. Had those same hands that now gestured expansively pushed Amelia off her cliff?

"I trust you find your lodging satisfactory," Vinny said, his voice smooth as expensive bourbon.

"It's incredible, Mr. Di Nuccio," Wolf replied, fighting to keep his voice steady.

"You're my guests here at the Stardust. Food, shows, whatever you desire—put it on your room tab." Vinny's smile was predatory. "Though if you feel lucky at the tables, that's your own business."

"Oh, we don't gamble," Carol said quickly.

"Smart policy," Vinny agreed, producing Elvis tickets with a magician's flourish. "The King's in town. Enjoy yourselves."

Wolf accepted the tickets with hands that he hoped weren't trembling. "Thank you for your generosity."

"My pleasure." Vinny's eyes glittered with something Wolf couldn't identify. "Now, did you bring me some Indians?"

Wolf's mouth felt like cotton as he opened the suitcase and removed two framed paintings—a Remington and an Eastman, both masterful forgeries that had taken weeks to complete. He propped them on the sofa, wondering if his artistic skills had somehow contributed to Amelia's death. Had his ability to create fake valuable art given Vinny ideas about her collection's worth?

Vinny's fingers traced the edge of the Remington. "This one looks fresh."

"It's designed to look like a century-old painting that's been recently restored," Wolf's voice sounded steadier than he felt.

"Explain."

Wolf turned to the Eastman, his hands moving with precision despite his inner turmoil. "This shows how a hundred years ages a painting—the yellowed varnish, the craquelure webbing. But the actual painting is only four weeks old."

Vinny leaned back, genuinely impressed. "Could have fooled me."

"It fooled the expert at Butterfield's Auction House. He valued it at two thousand, guaranteed."

"And the Remington?"

Wolf demonstrated the relining technique, explaining how restorers protected old canvases. "Butterfield's expert was impressed with the 'restoration work.' It adds significant value."

Vinny's smile was shark-like. "How does a kid like you get so damn sharp?"

"Wolfgang is a Certified Art Restorer trained in Europe," Carol said proudly, completely unaware of the danger radiating from their host.

Wolf felt sick. Carol's innocence was both her protection and her vulnerability. She had no idea she was praising a criminal to a man Wolf believed was a murderer.

"Carol, my dear," Vinny said smoothly, "would you mind if I borrowed Wolf for a private conversation?"

Carol's eyes flickered with uncertainty. "Of course."

"Excellent. Why don't you enjoy our spa while you wait? Third floor—ask for Margot. Tell her I want you to feel like a queen."

After Carol left, Vinny's demeanor shifted subtly. The gracious host facade remained, but something colder lurked beneath.

Vinny's office contained original art worth six figures. That is, Wolf thought the paintings were original. In Vinny's world, authenticity was just another negotiable commodity.

"I can't quite figure out your girlfriend's role in our little enterprise," Vinny began, circling Wolf like a predator sizing up prey.

Wolf's neck prickled with anger. "You mean my wife? Carol's with me. We don't keep secrets."

"Is that so?" Vinny's voice carried a subtle menace. "Does she know everything about your relationship with Amelia?"

The question caught Wolf off guard. This wasn't casual conversation. It was an interrogation about liability, about who knew what, about who might talk to the police.

"Not everything," Wolf admitted, hating how weak his voice sounded.

"Good. Keep it that way." Vinny's smile was arctic. "In this business, Wolf, ignorance is often the difference between a long life and a short one. Make sure Carol stays... uninformed about the details of our operations."

Wolf heard the threat clearly. "Understood."

"I hope so." Vinny settled behind his massive desk. "Now, let's discuss some practical matters. You won't be dealing directly with me anymore. Aaron Hudson at Las Vegas Antiques will be your contact. Bring him pieces like these, He'll give you cash. Clean, simple, safe."

Wolf nodded, though nothing about this felt safe.

"This Detective Stone from Laguna Beach," Vinny continued, "he's been very thorough in his investigation of poor Amelia's death. Asking about her art collection, her finances, her... associates."

Wolf's blood turned to ice. "What kind of questions?"

"The kind that suggests he knows more than he's letting on. The kind that could be very problematic for us." Vinny's gaze was laser-focused. "You wouldn't know anything about Amelia's death, would you?"

The question hung in the air like a noose. Was Vinny testing whether Wolf suspected him? Or was he genuinely trying to gauge Wolf's involvement?

"I know she owed you money," Wolf said carefully.

"Forty thousand dollars can weigh heavy on someone's mind," Vinny agreed. "Sometimes people do desperate things when they're cornered by debt. Sometimes they make poor decisions about where to walk on dark, stormy nights."

The way Vinny described it was so specific, so knowing, it made Wolf's skin crawl. Was that the voice of someone who'd been there? Who'd seen Amelia fall, or pushed her?

"She was found at the bottom of a cliff," Wolf managed.

"Tragic accident," Vinny replied, but his eyes remained cold and calculating. "Though the police seem to think otherwise. They're calling it murder now."

Wolf felt trapped between competing terrors. If he agreed, was he acknowledging Vinny's guilt? If he disagreed, was he covering for a killer?

"The investigation will probably focus on her personal relationships," Vinny continued. "Lovers, business partners, people who might have had access to her house on New Year's Eve."

The implicit threat was clear: Wolf had been Amelia's lover and business partner. He could easily become the prime suspect if Vinny decided to deflect attention.

"Art fraud is a federal crime," Vinny added casually. "Interstate commerce, you understand. The FBI takes a very dim view of people who flood the market with forgeries. Twenty-year sentences aren't uncommon."

Wolf realized he was caught in a perfect trap. If he tried to leave the operation, Vinny could frame him for Amelia's murder. If he stayed, he faced federal prison for art fraud. Either way, he was bound to a man he believed was a killer.

"New Year's Eve was a busy night," Vinny said thoughtfully. "Parties, celebrations, people out and about. Sometimes witnesses surface when you least expect them. The key is making sure they don't want to talk."

Wolf shuddered. Vinny wasn't just worried about the current investigation. He was prepared to silence anyone who might threaten their operation.

"I have a business proposition regarding Amelia's estate," Vinny continued. "Her daughter Julie is now responsible for my loan to Amelia. She will have to settle the debt before she can sell the house. I have a proposition for her. I'll cancel her mother's debt in exchange for the eight forgeries you painted for Amelia's collection. You think she'll go for it/"

"Hum…Julie doesn't know they're forgeries. She'll probably think those eight paintings are worth a lot more."

Exactly. That's why you're gonna have to come clean. Tell her what's what."

Wolf felt nauseous. "Her father, Howard Bloom, might be a problem," Wolf warned.

"Men like Bloom understand business. They know when to fight and when to accept a generous offer." Vinny's smile was reptilian. "Everyone can be made to see reason, Wolf. Everyone."

A s Wolf walked back to the suite, he realized he was trapped in a nightmare of his own making. He'd started as an artist looking for easy money and had become an accessory to what he believed was murder. Every successful forgery bound him tighter to Vinny, made him more complicit..

The police investigation was intensifying. Detective Stone was asking the right questions, and federal agents were reportedly interested in the art fraud angle. When the investigation finally connected Wolf to Amelia's death—whether as witness, accomplice, or fall guy—would Vinny let him live to testify?

Wolf thought about Carol, trusting and innocent, waiting for him in their luxury suite. She had no idea that her husband suspected their host of murder, or that their romantic criminal adventure was actually a death trap closing around them both.

The forgery operation that had promised freedom and wealth now felt like a prison built from his own greed and talent. Wolf was caught between a police investigation that could destroy him and a criminal partner who might kill him to protect the operation.

And Carol was trapped right alongside him, an innocent caught in a web of forgery, murder, and greed that was about to collapse around them all.

As Wolf reached for the door handle, he made a silent promise: whatever happened, he would find a way to protect Carol from the monster he'd made a deal with, even if it cost him his life\

37. THE RIGHT TO REMAIN SILENT

Ray Stone strode into the interview room in the bowels of Orange County jail, the familiar cocktail of disinfectant and desperation hitting him like a physical presence. The fluorescent light buzzed overhead, casting harsh shadows on the scarred metal table where Lenny Taubman sat cuffed, sweat beading on his forehead despite the room's chill.

Ray had been building toward this moment for weeks. The art theft had seemed like a random crime at first, but now he was certain it was the key that would unlock Amelia Hart's murder case.

"You're looking at serious time, Lenny," Ray said, settling into the hard chair across from the thief. "Parole violation, interstate transportation of stolen goods, conspiracy. The DA's talking about throwing the book at you."

Lenny shifted in his seat, the cuffs scraping against metal. "Look, Detective, I just took a painting. Nobody got hurt."

"That painting was stolen from a murder victim's estate," Ray said, watching Lenny's face carefully. "That makes you an accessory after the fact. Unless you want to tell me who really hired you."

Ray had done his homework. Lenny Taubman was a small-time thief with expensive habits and flexible morals. Exactly the kind of man someone like Jack Hart would use for dirty work.

"The guy said his name was Jack," Lenny finally admitted. "Said the painting needed to disappear."

Ray felt his pulse quicken but kept his expression neutral. "Describe him."

"White guy, maybe fifty, thinning hair. Talked like he had money. Real intense about politics, you know? Said the artist was spreading commie poison."

Ray slid Jack Hart's photograph across the table. "This him?"

Lenny studied the image, then nodded slowly. "Yeah, that's the guy."

There it was. Ray felt the familiar satisfaction of pieces clicking into place. Jack Hart hadn't just commissioned theft. He'd revealed his mindset toward Amelia. A man who believed traitors deserved punishment.

"What exactly did he say about Amelia Hart?" Ray pressed.

"Said she was using her art to spread anti-American poison. That she'd been stopped, but her propaganda needed to be destroyed too." Lenny's voice dropped. "Way he talked about her being 'stopped'... man was stone cold about it."

Ray made careful notes. This wasn't just evidence of art theft. It was proof of Jack's extremist hatred and his view of Amelia as an enemy who'd been permanently silenced.

Two hours later, Ray sat in his Ford outside the Orange County courthouse, reviewing Lenny's signed statement.

"Taubman's testimony gives us solid conspiracy charges for the art theft," Assistant DA Patricia Morrison had told him. "But for murder, we'll need Jack in custody to build the case."

Ray understood, but he was confident the murder case would come together once Jack was arrested. The art theft proved premeditation, that Jack had killed Amelia, then commissioned the theft to destroy evidence of his political motive.

As Ray drove back toward Laguna Beach, he felt the deep satisfaction that had been missing from his career since the LAPD debacle. This was real detective work—following evidence, building connections, solving a murder that could have gone cold.

By the time Ray reached Laguna Beach, he was ready to make the arrest that would close Amelia Hart's murder case.

Ray coordinated with Newport Beach PD as the sun set over Orange County. Detective Farnsworth confirmed backup would meet him at Jack Hart's Corona del Mar address. Ray checked his weapon, reviewed the arrest warrant, and felt the familiar pre-arrest adrenaline.

The Hart residence was a modest two-story house in an upscale neighborhood. Ray pulled up as the Newport Beach squad car arrived, its silent flashers painting the suburban street in alternating red and blue.

Together, they approached the front door. Ray knocked firmly, the sound echoing in the quiet evening air.

Jack Hart opened the door, his face shifting from mild curiosity to alarm as he registered the badges and uniforms. "Officers? What's this about?"

"Jack Hart, you're under arrest for the murder of Amelia

Hart," Ray said, producing his handcuffs. "You have the right to remain silent. Anything you say can and will be used against you in a court of law..."

As Ray recited the Miranda warning, Jack's shock seemed genuine, but Ray had learned not to trust appearances. Good killers were often good actors.

"Murder?" Jack's voice cracked. "I didn't murder anyone. This is insane."

"You have the right to an attorney," Ray continued. "If you cannot afford an attorney, one will be provided for you."

That's when the elderly woman, white-haired, fragile, leaning heavily on a walker, appeared behind Jack. Her face was a map of confusion and dawning terror.

"Jackie, who are these people? What's happening?"

Ray felt his chest tighten. This was a part of police work that never got easier—the collateral damage to innocent family members.

"Nothing to worry about, Mom," Jack said, his voice breaking. "Just a mistake."

"I'm sorry, ma'am, but your son needs to come with us," Ray said gently but firmly.

Her clouded eyes fixed on Ray with heartbreaking clarity. "But who will take care of me? Jackie takes care of me."

Ray felt the familiar conflict between duty and compassion. Julie Hart deserved justice for her mother's murder, even if it meant destroying another family in the process.

"Can I call a neighbor?" Jack asked, his political certainty crumbling into human frailty.

Ray nodded. "Quickly."

As Jack planned for his mother's care, Ray reflected on the case. The evidence was compelling: a political extremist with access kills a liberal artist, then covers his tracks by stealing her most provocative work.

The neighbor arrived, and Ray walked Jack to the patrol car in handcuffs, his mother's silhouette lingering in the doorway, a portrait of confusion and loss.

The drive back to Laguna Beach was quiet except for the engine's steady hum. Jack sat cuffed in the back seat, no longer the confident political warrior but a middle-aged man facing life in prison.

Ray felt the satisfaction he'd been chasing since his career imploded at LAPD. This was why he'd become a cop—to bring justice for victims like Amelia Hart.

"I didn't kill her," Jack said suddenly from the back seat.

Ray glanced in the rearview mirror. "Save it for your lawyer."

"I hated her politics, I'll admit that. But I didn't kill her."

Ray had heard the desperate protestations of innocence before from other criminals caught red-handed. "Your hired thief says otherwise. Says you told him Amelia had been 'stopped' and deserved what she got."

Jack fell silent, and Ray took that as confirmation. As they pulled into the Laguna Beach police station, Ray felt like a detective for the first time in months.

Ray completed the booking paperwork with careful attention to detail. Every procedure had to be perfect—Jack Hart had money for expensive lawyers who would exploit any mistake. But Ray was confident in his case.

As he locked up the evidence and headed home, Ray thought about calling Julie tomorrow with the good news. Her mother's killer was in custody, and the long nightmare of uncertainty was finally over.

He'd solved his first murder case since leaving LAPD, and he'd done it the right way—methodically, thoroughly, professionally. But something about Jack's silence in the backseat haunted Ray more than he expected. The man's shock had seemed genuine, and his denials carried a weight that felt different from the usual criminal protestations.

Ray pushed the doubt away. The evidence was solid. Jack Hart was a political extremist who saw Amelia as an enemy. Sometimes the obvious answer was the right answer. Still, as Ray drove through the quiet streets of Laguna Beach, he couldn't shake the feeling that something was missing from the picture he'd constructed. Something that would make all the pieces fit perfectly instead of just convincingly.

Tomorrow, he'd start building the murder case that would put Jack Hart away for life. Tonight, he'd try to ignore the small voice whispering that maybe, just maybe, he was missing something important.

38. A HOUSE MADE WHOLE

Mid-summer in Laguna Beach was an invitation to embrace the quintessential golden state of mind. The sun reigned supreme, casting a warm, amber hue that danced across the azure expanse of the Pacific. Days were long, and the air was saturated with a balmy heat that softened the edges of daily life.

But not today. Today, the news had shattered the peaceful afternoon like glass against stone.

Dennis sat beside Julie on her living room couch, his arm around her shoulders as she stared at the phone she'd just hung up. Detective Stone's words still echoed in the room: *Jack Hart has been arrested for the murder of Amelia Hart.*

"I can't believe it," Julie whispered, her voice barely audible. "I mean, I suspected... but to actually hear it."

Dennis felt her trembling against him. "How are you feeling?" he asked gently, knowing the question was inadequate for the complexity of emotions she must be experiencing.

She looked up at him, her eyes bright with unshed tears. "Relieved. Scared. Vindicated." She paused, searching for words. "Is it wrong that part of me feels... free?"

"No," Dennis said firmly. "It's not wrong at all. You've been living under a shadow of suspicion and fear. Now you know the truth."

Julie leaned into him, and he could feel some of the tension leave her body. "The detective said they found evidence in his apartment. Physical evidence linking him to..." She couldn't finish the sentence.

Dennis's protective instincts surged alongside his journalistic curiosity, but he pushed the latter aside. This wasn't a story. It was Julie's life, her trauma, her healing. "You don't have to think about the details right now," he said softly.

"I should call my father," Julie said suddenly, sitting up straighter. "He needs to know. And... Dennis, I know this changes things, but would you still be willing to meet him? I think I need both of you here right now."

Dennis squeezed her hand. "Of course. Whatever you need."

That evening, the time came for introductions under circumstances Dennis could never have imagined. At first glance, Howard Bloom reminded Dennis of Robert Mitchum, with his hooded eyes and relaxed demeanor, accentuated by his deep voice and slow, deliberate way of speaking. But tonight, concern for his daughter etched deeper lines around his eyes.

Dennis felt the moment's weight as if it had settled onto his shoulders, though now it came from more than just meeting Julie's father—they were all processing the day's shocking revelation. As the man's gaze met his, Dennis saw both scrutiny and gratitude there.

Dennis extended his hand, the light from the antique lamp

glinting off his watch. "It's a pleasure to meet you, Mr. Bloom, though I wish it were under better circumstances."

Mr. Bloom's grip was firm, his hand enveloping Dennis's with an easy strength. A weary smile crinkled the corners of his eyes. "Please, call me Howie," he said, releasing Dennis's hand and gesturing toward the plush armchair across from him. "Julie's told me quite a bit about you, and I'm grateful she has your support during all this." He studied Dennis's face. "You look like you're carrying the weight of the world. You're here for my daughter."

Dennis sank into the armchair, the leather cool against his back. "I care about her very much, sir. Today's been overwhelming for all of us, I imagine."

Howie leaned forward, his elbows resting on his knees, his gaze direct but kind. "It has been. But I have to say, your articles about Amelia were excellent. They captured who she really was as a person and an artist. That means something, especially now."

"Thank you," Dennis said. "I felt a responsibility to tell her story accurately. She deserved that."

"She did." Howie's expression grew more serious. "Dennis, I have to ask. What's your impression of Jack Hart? Julie's told me some things, but you've been investigating this case. Did you suspect him?"

Dennis chose his words carefully. "There were inconsistencies in his story from the beginning. His behavior toward Julie after Amelia's death raised red flags. The way he tried to control the narrative, pressure Julie about the house." He glanced toward the kitchen, where Julie was making coffee. "I was concerned about Julie's safety, to be honest."

Howie nodded grimly. "I never liked him. There was always something calculating about Jack, even when Amelia married his father. But I never imagined..." He shook his head. "What kind of man kills someone over politics?"

"The kind who sees people as objects to be manipulated," Dennis replied. "Amelia trusted him. She probably never saw it coming."

"Julie blames herself," Howie said quietly. "She thinks she should have protected Amelia somehow."

"That's not her burden to carry," Dennis said with conviction. "Jack fooled everyone. Even the police initially focused elsewhere."

Howie studied Dennis with a new interest. "You really care about her."

"I do," Dennis said simply. "More than I expected to when we first met."

Julie's voice drifted from the kitchen as she spoke on the phone, her tone a mixture of relief and exhaustion as she updated someone about the arrest.

"This changes everything for her," Howie said. "Her sense of safety, her ability to move forward."

Dennis nodded. "She's stronger than she knows. But she shouldn't have to face this alone."

"No," Howie agreed, "she shouldn't. And I'm glad she doesn't have to."

The approval in his voice was unmistakable, and Dennis felt some of his own tension ease. It wasn't just about meeting Julie's father anymore. It was about being accepted into a family circle during its time of crisis.

Julie appeared in the doorway with a tray of coffee, her composure more settled than it had been hours earlier. "Are you two bonding over my dramatic life?" she asked with a weak smile.

"We're discussing what an extraordinary woman you are," Howie said, reaching for her hand as she set down the tray.

"And how proud we are of your strength," Dennis added.

Julie's eyes filled with tears, but they were tears of gratitude rather than fear.

As the evening progressed, the conversation turned to practical matters. Julie had been quiet for several minutes, her hands wrapped around her coffee mug, when she suddenly looked up at her father.

"Dad, can we talk?" she asked, her eyes beckoning Howie toward the kitchen.

Dennis remained in the living room, giving them privacy but unable to avoid overhearing their conversation in the open-plan space.

"Dad, with everything that's happened today, I've been thinking about the house." Julie's voice held a blend of determination and vulnerability. "I know we talked about refinancing before, but now, with Jack arrested, I feel like I can finally breathe here again. This place feels like home, not a crime scene."

Howie's response was measured, his bass voice audible from the kitchen. "Julie, I understand what this house means to you, especially now. But think practically. You're just starting your life, you could use the liquid assets more than trying to maintain a big house like this."

Dennis heard the soft clink of a cup being set down. There was a pause, and then Julie spoke again, her voice rising with emotion.

"I am thinking practically, Dad. This place isn't just home. It's stability. It's proof that I can build something good from all this chaos. The refinancing is doable, especially now that I don't have to worry about Jack trying to sabotage me."

A sigh was audible from Howie. "The arrest changes things, I'll give you that. But refinancing means taking on debt, and your income from freelance photography is..."

"Not steady," Julie interrupted. "Dennis feels there might be renewed interest in Amelia's work now that there's closure to her story. I could organize a memorial exhibition."

Dennis felt a warmth at being included in her plans, at being part of her support system rather than just a witness to her struggles.

Julie continued, her voice softening. "Dad, if I sell now, it feels like Jack wins. Like he gets to disrupt my life one more time. I need this house. I need to prove to myself that I can hold onto something beautiful."

When Howie next spoke, his voice held less resistance. "What about the emotional associations? Won't living here remind you of... everything?"

"It already has been," Julie said. "But today, when I heard about Jack's arrest, I felt something shift. This house was never the problem. Jack was. And now he can't hurt anyone anymore."

Dennis rose from his seat, compelled to move closer, offering silent support as Julie reached for her father's hands.

"Please, Dad," she implored with an earnest gaze. "This home represents my fresh start. With Jack out of the picture, I can make it mine completely. I just need you to trust me."

Howie looked into his daughter's eyes, seeing a determination and clarity that perhaps hadn't been there before the day's revelations. Dennis watched as his resolve wavered, the decision hanging in the balance.

"The arrest does change the financial picture," Howie

admitted slowly. "And if you're certain this is what you want..."

"It is," Julie said firmly. "For the first time in months, I know exactly what I want."

Howie's weathered hands covered hers. "Then we'll make it work. You've been through enough upheaval. If keeping this house gives you peace, then that's what we'll do."

Julie's face lit up with relief and gratitude. Dennis felt his chest tighten with emotion—not just at her joy, but at being present for this moment of family support and new beginnings.

As father and daughter embraced, Dennis realized he was witnessing more than just a financial decision. He was seeing Julie reclaim her life, her space, her future—with both her father's support and, he hoped, with him by her side.

The arrest that had shattered their afternoon had, by evening's end, cleared the way for something Dennis sensed would be much stronger than what came before.

39. ECHOES FROM THE BLUFF

Ray Stone leaned back in his desk chair, the phone pressed to his ear as Maggie's laughter filtered through the receiver. For the first time in months, he felt the satisfaction of a case well solved. Jack Hart was in custody, the evidence was solid, and the DA was confident about prosecution.

"So the great detective finally gets his man," Maggie teased, her voice warm with affection.

Ray's grin widened. "What can I say? Sometimes the good guys win." He was about to suggest dinner to celebrate when O'Neil's face appeared over the cubicle partition, his expression cutting through Ray's good mood like a blade.

"Ray, you're gonna want to see this," O'Neil said, his voice carrying an undertone that made Ray's stomach clench. "Interview Room One. Now."

"Babe, something's come up. I'll call you back," Ray muttered into the phone, his celebratory mood evaporating as he followed O'Neil's urgent stride.

The walk down the hallway felt longer than usual, each step weighted with growing dread. O'Neil's shoulders were tense, and he kept glancing back at Ray with an expression that looked almost apologetic.

The door to Interview Room One opened to reveal a scene that made Ray's chest tighten. Two adults stood protectively behind a pair of teenagers who looked like they were carrying the weight of the world. The kids couldn't have been more than sixteen or seventeen, their faces pale and drawn.

"Detective Stone handles the Amelia Hart case," O'Neil said, his voice carefully neutral as he made the introduction.

The adults immediately began speaking over each other until the man gestured for the woman to continue. She stepped forward, her knuckles white as she gripped her daughter's shoulder.

"Detective, I'm Sara Pierson. This is my daughter, Allison." Her voice was steady, but Ray could see the tremor in her hands. "And this is Jim Henderson and his son Jake."

Ray felt his detective instincts kick in even as confusion swirled in his mind. "What can I help you folks with?"

The girl, Allison, looked up for the first time, her eyes red-rimmed but determined. When she spoke, her voice was barely above a whisper, but each word landed like a physical blow.

"We saw Mrs. Hart fall to her death at Pirate's Cove."

The room seemed to tilt. Ray felt his carefully constructed case beginning to crumble before he even understood why. He gripped the back of a chair, fighting to keep his expression neutral.

"And when was this?" His voice sounded distant to his own ears.

"New Year's Eve," Allison replied, then quickly looked back down at her hands.

Ray stood in stunned silence, his mind racing. Jack Hart

had been arrested based on months of investigation, physical evidence, and witness statements. And now two kids were sitting in his interview room, claiming they saw an accident?

"I need you to tell me exactly what you saw," Ray said slowly, sinking into a chair across from them. "Take your time."

Jake glanced at his father, who nodded encouragingly, then began to speak. His voice cracked slightly with nerves. "We... we were down on the beach. Pirate Beach, you know? The little hidden one by the point north of Shaw's Cove."

"We weren't supposed to be there," Allison interrupted, shooting a guilty look at her mother. "We were supposed to be at Becky Miller's New Year's party."

"I talked her into coming with me," Jake said quickly. "It wasn't her fault. I took my dad's boat without permission." He swallowed hard. "We just wanted somewhere quiet to hang out, you know? We built a fire and were just... talking."

Ray nodded, his pen moving automatically across his notepad even though part of his mind was screaming that this couldn't be happening. "Go on."

"That's when we heard the yelling," Allison continued, her voice getting stronger. "This woman was at the top of the stairs, screaming at us to get off her property. She was throwing rocks down at us."

"Rocks?" Ray's pen stopped moving.

"Yeah, like, good-sized ones," Jake said. "She was really angry, calling us trespassers and... worse things. She sounded drunk. Her words were all slurred, and she was swaying around up there."

Ray felt sweat beading on his forehead. "What happened next?"

"I yelled back that she didn't own the beach," Jake admitted, his cheeks reddening. "I know I shouldn't have, but we weren't doing anything wrong. We were just sitting by our fire."

"The tide was coming in anyway," Allison added. "We were getting ready to leave when she... when she fell."

"Tell me about the fall," Ray said, his voice hoarse.

Allison's eyes filled with tears. "She was leaning over the railing, screaming at us and throwing another rock. She lost her balance and just... went over. She hit her head on the way down and landed on the rocks at the bottom of the stairs."

The room was dead silent except for the hum of the fluorescent lights overhead. Ray could hear his own heartbeat in his ears.

"Did you try to help her?" he managed to ask.

"Of course we did," Jake said, his voice defensive. "We ran over to her right away, but she was already..." He swallowed hard. "There was blood on the rocks. Her neck was twisted funny. She was gone."

Ray set down his pen and rubbed his temples, feeling a headache building behind his eyes. "Why didn't you report this immediately?"

The parents exchanged glances, and Sara Pierson spoke up. "They were terrified, Detective. Two kids who weren't supposed to be there, a woman dead, and they thought they'd be blamed."

"We panicked," Allison whispered. "We got in the boat and went home. We told our parents we'd been at the party all night."

"And you've kept this secret for six months?" Ray asked, though he already knew the answer.

Jake nodded miserably. "We thought... we thought it would just be ruled an accident and that would be it. We didn't know it would become a murder investigation."

"So why come forward now?" Ray's question hung heavy in the air.

Allison looked up at him with tears streaming down her face. "Because we heard on the news that a man was arrested. I couldn't sleep, couldn't eat. I kept thinking about him sitting in jail for something he didn't do." Her voice broke. "I finally told my mom yesterday."

Ray pushed back from the table and stood up, his legs feeling unsteady. "I need a few minutes to process this. Officers will take your formal statements."

He walked out of the interview room on autopilot, his mind reeling. Six months of investigation. Physical evidence. Witness interviews. A solid case against Jack Hart. And it was all wrong.

The squad room was nearly empty, the day shift having departed hours ago. Ray moved like a man underwater, pulling the thick Amelia Hart file from the cabinet with hands that trembled slightly. The Manila folder felt heavier than it should have, weighted with months of wrong assumptions and false conclusions.

He flipped through the pages until he found what he was looking for—the medical examiner's report. That damn chlorine finding that had convinced him Amelia had drowned in her pool before being moved to the ocean. The detail that had made him certain this was murder.

Ray picked up his phone and dialed the ME's office.

"Doc, it's Ray Stone. You remember the Amelia Hart case from New Year's?"

"The artist from Laguna? Sure. What about it?"

Ray closed his eyes, feeling the words stick in his throat.

"I've got two eyewitnesses who say they saw her fall accidentally from the bluff at Shaw's Cove."

There was a pause on the other end. "Okay... so what's the question?"

"The chlorine you found in her lungs. I assumed it meant she drowned in a pool first, but..." Ray rubbed his forehead. "She was a regular swimmer. Could she have had chlorine in her system just from normal pool use?"

The ME's voice was patient, professional. "Absolutely. Regular swimmers, especially those who do laps in chlorinated pools, often have detectable levels of chlorine and chloramines in their respiratory system. It's actually quite common."

Ray felt the last pillar of his case crumble. "So finding chlorine doesn't necessarily indicate drowning?"

"Not at all. In fact, given her swimming habits, I'd have been more surprised not to find traces of chlorine."

Ray hung up the phone and stared at the file spread across his desk. Every piece of evidence he'd thought pointed to murder could be explained by accident. The head trauma was from hitting the rocks during the fall. The positioning of the body from the tide moving her. Even the chlorine that had seemed so significant.

Six months. Six goddamn months chasing shadows while the truth was sitting in two kids' guilty consciences.

Ray leaned back in his chair, the empty squad room echoing with the weight of his realization. The fluorescent lights hummed overhead, casting harsh shadows across the scattered case files.

I was so sure. So convinced I was following the evidence where it led. But I wasn't following evidence—I was following assumptions. I took that chlorine finding and built an entire murder case around it because that's what I wanted to see.

The taste in his mouth was bitter, like he'd been chewing on regret for hours. It wasn't just about being wrong, because every detective got cases wrong sometimes. I was about how wrong he'd been, how completely he'd constructed an alternate reality based on flawed reasoning.

Jack Hart. Son of a bitch is probably guilty of being a political nutjob and a greedy bastard, but not murder. And he's sitting in county lockup right now because I was too proud of my instincts to consider simpler explanations.

Ray picked up a pen and began writing his report, each word feeling like a small defeat. But even as he documented his failure, part of his mind was already working differently. More carefully. More skeptically—including skepticism about his own conclusions.

The thing about being a detective is that every case teaches you something. Some lessons come easy, from watching other cops make mistakes or getting lucky breaks. And some lessons, the ones that really stick, come from getting your ass handed to you by a couple of scared teenagers who finally found the courage to tell the truth.

He thought about calling Maggie back, about having to explain why their celebration dinner would have to be postponed indefinitely. About the paperwork tsunami that was about to hit. About facing the press in the morning.

But mostly he thought about those kids in Interview Room One, who'd carried this secret for six months until their consciences finally wouldn't let them stay quiet. They'd shown more integrity in the end than he had throughout his entire investigation.

Next time, and there's always a next time, I'm going to remember this feeling. The sick weight of being completely, utterly wrong. I'm going to remember that evidence tells a story, but investigators choose how to read it. And I'm going to choose more carefully.

Ray closed the file and locked it back in the cabinet. Tomorrow, he'd start the process of undoing months of work, of freeing an innocent man and officially closing the case as accidental death. Tonight, he'd sit with the hard-earned knowledge that experience and instinct weren't enough if they weren't paired with intellectual humility.

The squad room was quiet, but Ray's mind was already preparing for the next case, the next test of everything he thought he knew about being a detective. This time, he'd be ready.

40. FREEDOM, SIGNED
   IN INK

Julie had been dreading this call for months. Every time the phone rang, every unexpected knock at the door, she wondered if it would be Vincent Di Nuccio coming to collect. The forty-thousand-dollar debt had hung over her like a storm cloud, and she knew that eventually, the rain would come.

She was chopping romaine for dinner, trying to lose herself in the mundane rhythm of food prep, when the phone's sharp ring cut through her fragile peace. Her knife paused mid-chop, and she felt her stomach clench with familiar dread.

"Please don't be him," she whispered to herself as she wiped her hands on her apron and reached for the receiver.

"Miss Bloom? Vincent Di Nuccio here."

Her worst fear materialized in those four words. Julie gripped the phone tighter, her knuckles going white against the black plastic.

"My condolences about Amelia," he continued, his voice carrying a warmth that somehow made it more unsettling. "Real tragedy, losing someone like that. She was…special."

"Thank you, Mr. Di Nuccio." Julie's voice came out steadier

than she felt, though her free hand trembled as she reached for the counter's edge.

"Now, I know this is a difficult time, but there's a matter we need to discuss. Your mother and I had a business arrangement. Proper paperwork, promissory note. Amelia insisted on doing everything legal and aboveboard."

Julie closed her eyes, bracing herself. *Here it comes.*

"I loaned her forty thousand about a year back. Now with circumstances being what they are..." He paused, and Julie could almost hear his shrug through the phone. "Well, a debt's a debt, even when it's family."

"I... yes, I'm aware of the loan." Julie's mouth felt dry. "But Mr. Di Nuccio, I don't have that kind of money."

"Course you don't, sweetheart. Nobody expects you to have forty grand lying around." His chuckle was soft, almost paternal. "But Amelia, she was smart. She offered me something else instead—eight paintings. Said they were reproductions, but beautiful work. Art for art's sake, you know?"

Julie's breath caught. He knows they're reproductions. Relief and terror warred in her chest.

"Now, I'm not saying this to pressure you," Di Nuccio continued, though they both knew that was exactly what he was doing. "But the promissory note's recorded proper, and there's a lien on your property. I'm hoping we can handle this like civilized people."

Julie's mind raced, but something in her, something that had been growing stronger over the past months, refused to crumble.

"I need to speak with my attorney before I can discuss this further," she said, surprised by the firmness in her own voice.

There was a pause. Then Di Nuccio's laugh, genuine this time. "Smart girl. Amelia raised you right. Take your time,

Miss Bloom. But not too much time, if you catch my meaning."

The line went dead, and Julie stood frozen in her kitchen for one moment of pure panic. Then she straightened her shoulders and dialed her father.

H owie's voice carried surprise and concern. "He actually used the word 'reproductions'?"

"Yes, and he mentioned a promissory note. Dad, is this lien legitimate?"

"If Amelia signed proper paperwork, then yes. But Julie, you need legal representation. Call your accountant and get a referral for someone local."

Julie felt tears prick her eyes. "These are Amelia's paintings, Dad. Her legacy."

"Her legacy is the woman she helped raise," Howie said firmly. "You know what she'd want you to choose."

T he law office of Stuart Anders occupied the ground floor of a Spanish-style building in downtown Laguna. Julie sat in an oversized leather chair, her palms sweating as she waited.

Anders was middle-aged with kind eyes behind wire-rimmed glasses, not the intimidating legal eagle she'd imagined.

"Ms. Bloom, I've reviewed the documents," he said, settling behind his desk. "The promissory note was properly notarized and recorded. Mr. Di Nuccio has legal grounds for the lien."

Julie's heart sank. "So I have to pay him?"

"Not necessarily. The art transfer option gives you a clean

resolution. Once both parties sign the settlement agreement and the paintings are transferred, the lien gets removed from your property." Anders leaned forward, his expression serious but kind. "The question is: what do you want the outcome to be?"

Julie stared out the window at the afternoon light filtering through the pepper trees. What did she want? Freedom. Peace of mind. The ability to move forward.

"I want this to be over," she said finally. "I want to sleep at night without wondering when he's going to show up at my door."

Anders nodded. "Then let's make that happen."

Twenty minutes later, Julie signed the settlement agreement, each signature feeling like a small act of liberation. When it was done, Anders shook her hand with a smile.

"Congratulations, Ms. Bloom. Once Mr. Di Nuccio signs and the art transfer is completed, you'll be free and clear."

Julie stepped out into the afternoon light, and for the first time in months, she could breathe fully.

She found a payphone on the corner, its red paint faded but functional. The glass booth felt like a private sanctuary as she closed herself inside and dialed her father's number.

"Dad, it's me." Her voice broke slightly on the words.

"Julie? How did it go?"

"It's done. The papers are signed. Once Di Nuccio completes his part, the lien is gone." She pressed her forehead against the cool glass. "I'm going to be free."

"Oh, kiddo." Howie's voice was thick with emotion. "I'm so proud of you."

"It doesn't feel heroic, giving away Amelia's paintings."

"Sometimes the most heroic thing we can do is save ourselves," Howie said gently. "Amelia would understand."

Julie wiped her eyes, surprised to find them wet with tears of relief so profound it felt like grief for the fear she was finally letting go.

"For months, everything has been about just surviving. Now, for the first time, I can actually think about the future."

"And what do you see?"

Julie looked through the phone booth glass at the busy street, at people walking with purpose and joy, at the endless California sky. "Possibilities," she said. "I see possibilities."

When she hung up and stepped out of the booth, the late afternoon sun felt warm on her face. The tightness in her shoulders that had been her constant companion for months was finally beginning to ease.

For the first time since Amelia's death, Julie felt like herself again. Not the frightened woman who had discovered a body, not the suspect in a murder investigation, not the debtor hiding from collectors. Just Julie—free to choose her own path forward.

As she drove home through the winding streets of Laguna Beach, past the art galleries and ocean views that had become part of her identity, she realized she was ready for whatever came next.

She was finally, completely, her own person.

41. THE ARTIST AND
THE DEBT

Wolf's hands trembled as he reached for the phone. Six months since Amelia's death, living under the weight of suspicion, and only today had the police finally closed the case. He dialed the number that connected him to a world of threats disguised as favors.

"Yeah?" Di Nuccio's gravelly voice cut through the line after two rings.

"Vinny, it's Wolf." He cleared his throat, trying to steady his voice. "There's news about Amelia."

A pause. Wolf could almost hear the man's calculating mind spinning. "What kind of news?"

"The police closed the case. It wasn't murder." Wolf gripped the phone tighter. "Two kids saw her fall from the cliff. It was an accident. They just came forward."

"No shit? Took 'em long enough."

"They were scared. They weren't supposed to be there."

"Well, well. That's convenient for everybody, ain't it?" Di Nuccio's chuckle held no warmth. "Speaking of convenient, I just got off the phone with Amelia's girl. Sweet kid, that Julie.

We worked out our little arrangement about those paintings you made for Amelia."

Wolf's stomach clenched. The eight forgeries—a Pissarro, two Fattori, a Liebermann, and four others. Each one is a noose tightening around his neck. "The collection?"

"That's right. Julie thinks they're just copies Amelia commissioned for her personal collection. Nice kid, paying off her mother's debts like that. Jimmy's gonna pick them up tomorrow, ten a.m. sharp. Where do you want them delivered?"

"My house. The studio's too public now, too many people coming and going since..." He let the sentence hang.

"Good thinking. And Wolf?" Di Nuccio's voice dropped lower, intimate and threatening. "I know what you're thinking. Case closed, debt settled, maybe it's time to renegotiate our arrangement."

Wolf's heart hammered against his ribs. *Was I that transparent?*

"The thing is," Di Nuccio continued, "nothing's changed between you and me. You keep doing those restoration jobs I send your way, and I keep making sure nobody asks questions about where Amelia's originals really came from. You stop working for me, and I make sure the FBI knows who really painted those plein air masterpieces. Simple arrangement. We got a good thing going. That's what we agreed on. Period."

Wolf realized he'd been holding his breath. He exhaled slowly, the sound audible in the silence. "I understand."

"I hope you do because I'd hate for there to be any... misunderstandings. About what you created. About who knew what and when."

The line went dead.

Wolf stood frozen, the dial tone buzzing in his ear. He hung up slowly, his hand shaking as he set the receiver in its cradle. The gallery felt smaller now, the air heavy with linseed oil and old varnish. He'd thought Amelia's accidental death might free him. Instead, it had sealed the cage. Before, he could tell himself he was protecting her secrets, honoring their partnership. Now he was simply trapped.

The studio door opened with its familiar creak, and Carol slipped inside, carrying bags of Chinese takeout. The rich aroma of garlic and ginger filled the space, but Wolf's stomach was still churning.

"You look terrible," Carol said, setting the bags on the worktable. She studied his face, and her expression shifted from concern to recognition. "Di Nuccio."

Wolf nodded.

She was quiet for a moment, unpacking containers with deliberate care. "What did he want?"

"Jimmy's coming tomorrow at ten to pick up the eight paintings at Amelia's house. I told him to deliver them at the house." Wolf began clearing space on the table, grateful for something to do with his hands. "Can you make sure you're somewhere else when he arrives?"

"I'll visit my sister." Carol's voice was flat. She handed him chopsticks, then met his eyes. "Did you tell him about Amelia's case?"

"Yes."

"And he's letting you go?"

Wolf laughed, a bitter sound. "He made it very clear I'm more useful to him now than ever."

Carol set down her container, her appetite apparently gone. "Wolf, I need to know something." She paused, choosing her words carefully. "When this all started with Di Nuccio. Did you think about us? About what would happen if you got caught?"

The question landed like a physical blow. Wolf looked at his wife, really looked at her. The fine lines around her eyes hadn't been there five years ago. The tension in her shoulders never fully relaxed anymore. The way she held herself at a slight distance, as if proximity to him might contaminate her.

"Every day," he said quietly. "I think about it every day."

"But not before. Not when it mattered."

It wasn't an accusation. It was worse. It was a statement of fact, delivered with the weariness of someone who'd stopped expecting better.

Carol stood, gathering the barely-touched containers. "I have invoices to finish. We still have a legitimate business to run." She paused at the door. "Lock up when you leave. And Wolf? Tomorrow, when Jimmy comes, I don't want to know anything about it. Not where the paintings go, not what happens to them. Nothing."

The door closed behind her with a soft click.

Alone now, Wolf locked the door and moved to the window. Somewhere out there, Julie Bloom was probably relieved, thinking she'd settled her mother's debts with eight paintings she believed were legitimate copies. She had no idea each canvas was a felony.

And Wolf couldn't tell her the truth without destroying himself.

He turned back to his studio, seeing it with the harsh clarity that came from his conversation with Carol. The space was cluttered—tubes of paint scattered across the worktable, brushes soaking in cloudy jars of turpentine, drop cloths stained with years of color. On the east wall hung his own work: a seascape he'd painted last month, bold and alive with light. Near it, a half-finished street scene, pure and uncompromising. His vision, untainted.

Across the room, three "restorations" in various stages of completion leaned against the opposite wall. A Renoir garden scene. A Degas dancer. A Cézanne landscape. Each one technically perfect, meticulously aged, utterly false. Di Nuccio's commissions.

Wolf walked to the Renoir and studied it in the dim light. The brushwork was flawless—he'd matched every stroke, every color shift, every subtle gradation. It was perhaps the finest technical work he'd ever done. It was also a lie that would hang in some collector's home, appreciated for genius that wasn't his own.

His cigarette pack sat on the worktable. Wolf lit one and let the smoke fill his lungs, the familiar burn almost comforting. His neck ached from tension. His eyes felt gritty with exhaustion. His hands—his talented, compromised hands—were stained with cadmium yellow that wouldn't wash out.

The studio's ventilation system hummed its constant white noise. Outside, waves crashed against the rocks below, rhythmic and indifferent. The overhead fluorescents cast everything in harsh, honest light—no shadows to hide in, no soft edges to blur the truth of what he'd become.

On his easel sat a canvas he'd stretched and primed last week, before the world had shifted again. It waited, blank and patient.

Wolf crushed out his cigarette and stood. Tomorrow, Jimmy would come for the paintings. Tomorrow, Di Nuccio's hold would tighten further. Tomorrow he'd wake up still trapped, still painting lies for ugly men who trafficked in beauty they couldn't create themselves.

But tonight, just for tonight, he could choose what went on that canvas.

Wolf selected a brush from the jar, wiped it clean, and tested its spring against his palm. He studied his palette—the colors he'd mixed for his own work, not Di Nuccio's. Cobalt blue. Cadmium red. Titanium white. Simple, honest pigments.

He dipped the brush in the blue and approached the canvas. For a moment, he hesitated. Then he made the first stroke, a bold sweep of color across the white surface. Not careful. Not calculated. Just true.

In the morning, he'd go back to being what Di Nuccio needed him to be. But for these few hours, in this cluttered studio above the Pacific, with paint-stained hands and borrowed time, he could still remember what it felt like to be an artist.

Wolf made another stroke, then another. The painting began to emerge—something his, something real.

It would have to be enough.

42. BENEATH THE SURFACE

Julie stood in her sun-drenched living room, eight paintings leaning against the cream-colored wall. Vincent Di Nuccio's man, Jimmy, would arrive within the hour to collect them—the final step in freeing herself from the forty-thousand-dollar debt that had haunted her since Amelia's death.

She moved closer to examine them one last time, coffee mug warming her hands. They were beautiful. Wolf's technical skill was undeniable. But something about them felt wrong, though she couldn't name it until now.

These weren't Wolf's usual work.

The painting closest to the window caught her attention—a woman in a garden, dappled sunlight filtering through leaves. The style was unmistakably Impressionist, the brushwork loose and luminous. In the corner, a signature: *Berthe Morisot, 1878.*

Julie set down her mug and tilted the canvas to catch the light. The surface showed subtle craquelure—fine cracks in the paint and varnish that came from decades of expansion and contraction. The canvas itself had the slight sag of age, and the stretcher bars showed wear at the corners.

She examined the next painting—a mother and child, the tender intimacy characteristic of Mary Cassatt. Then a street scene that had to be Pissarro, all bustling energy and atmospheric perspective. A Sisley river landscape. A Renoir garden party. A second Cassatt, this one of a woman at her toilette. Two more smaller pieces—a Guillaumin and a Monet harbor scene.

Eight Impressionist masterpieces she'd never seen before. A famous artist signed each one. Each one showed the patina of genuine age.

Vincent had told her these were high-quality reproductions Amelia had commissioned for her personal study. But reproductions weren't signed with the original artist's name and date. Reproductions weren't aged to look like period pieces. Reproductions were marked as copies, signed by the artist who made them, and sold openly as tributes or learning exercises.

These weren't reproductions. These were meant to pass as real.

Julie's hands had gone cold despite the warm California morning. She pulled Amelia's magnifying loupe from the drawer where she'd stored her mother's appraisal tools. She'd spent the last three months learning to use it, cataloging Amelia's collection for the estate, remembering everything Amelia had taught her about examining paintings—lessons that had seemed academic until now.

Under magnification, her suspicion crystallized into certainty.

The craquelure was too uniform. Real aging created random patterns—cracks that followed stress points in the canvas, areas of heavy paint application, and environmental damage accumulated over decades. These cracks were too methodical, like a pattern stamped onto the surface rather than damage earned through time. They followed the weave of the canvas rather than the natural stresses of the paint layer.

She checked another painting. Same pattern. Then another. All eight showed the same artificial aging, the same deliberate distressing.

But underneath the false age, she could see Wolf's hand. The way he caught light on fabric—she'd watched him demonstrate that technique. His specific way of building up texture in foliage, leaving slight impasto where Impressionists would have used thinner paint. The precise pressure of his brush in highlights, a signature habit she'd noticed during their lessons together over the past year.

Wolf had painted these. Recently. And someone had aged them to look like lost masterpieces from the 1870s and 1880s.

Julie's stomach tightened. She thought of Amelia's casual comments about the art market. *"Provenance is everything, darling. A painting is only worth what someone can prove it is."* Another time, reviewing auction catalogs: *"So many pieces were lost during the wars. Sometimes things surface that have been hidden in private collections for decades. No one questions them if the story is right."*

Had Amelia been preparing her? Or warning her?

Julie grabbed the Polaroid camera from the hall closet—the one she'd been using to document pieces from Amelia's collection for the estate inventory. Her hands shook as she photographed the Morisot, making sure to capture the signature and the telltale uniformity of the craquelure. The image slid out, and she set it carefully on the side table to develop, trying to shield it from direct sunlight.

She was lining up the second shot on the Cassatt when she heard the truck in the driveway.

No. Not yet.

She snapped the photo quickly, fumbling with the camera as the second image emerged. The truck door slammed outside.

Julie shoved the camera back in the closet and grabbed the first Polaroid. It had developed enough—grainy and imperfect, but it showed what she'd seen. She slipped both photos into her purse just as the knock came, her heart hammering.

"Miss Bloom?" Jimmy's voice was firm but professional. "I'm here for the pickup."

Julie opened the door, trying to keep her face neutral. Jimmy filled the doorway—heavyset, work clothes, the kind of face that was hard to read. He held up a clipboard with practiced efficiency.

"Afternoon, Miss Bloom. Got your paperwork here. Just confirming the eight pieces as agreed upon."

Julie signed with fingers that felt numb. She watched as he methodically loaded the paintings into padded cases he'd brought, his movements practiced and careful. This wasn't some amateur operation. This was professional, systematic, which somehow made it more terrifying.

"These are remarkable pieces," Jimmy commented as he wrapped the Morisot, then glanced at her. "Mr. Di Nuccio has very particular buyers lined up."

The way he said it—watching her face as he spoke—made Julie's skin prickle. Did he know she'd figured it out? Was he testing her?

"I'm sure he does," she managed.

"Mr. Di Nuccio wanted me to tell you the lien paperwork should be finalized by the end of the week," Jimmy said, checking items off his list. "You're free and clear, Miss Bloom. Your mother's debt is settled."

"Thank you," Julie said, though the words felt hollow.

After Jimmy left, Julie stood in the empty living room for a long moment, staring at the wall where the paintings had been. The morning sunlight slanted across the vacant space, highlighting dust motes in the air.

She walked to the couch and sat, pulling the two Polaroids from her purse. They were grainy, imperfect—far from the quality of documentation a real investigation would need. But they showed what she'd seen: Wolf's brushwork hidden beneath false signatures, artificial aging masquerading as authenticity.

Eight forged Impressionist paintings, now on their way to "particular buyers" who would pay enormous sums for what they believed were lost masterpieces. And she'd just handed them over, signed the paperwork, made herself part of whatever scheme this was.

Julie thought about Wolf—patient Wolf who'd spent hours teaching her about composition and color theory, who'd shown her how to see the temperature of light. "Don't paint what you think you see," he'd told her, his hands guiding her brush. "Paint what's actually there."

Had he been lying even then? Or had Amelia trapped him the way Di Nuccio had trapped her?

She picked up the phone and dialed Dennis's number.

"Julie? What's wrong?"

"Dennis, I need to ask you something." She took a breath. "What do you know about art forgery?"

A pause. "Art forgery? What kind of question is that?"

"The paintings I just gave to Di Nuccio." Julie's voice wavered. "They weren't what Vincent said they were. They weren't reproductions for personal study. They were—Dennis, I think they were forgeries. Real ones. Meant to be sold as authentic Impressionist paintings."

The silence on the other end stretched long. When Dennis spoke again, his voice had changed—quieter, more careful.

"Jesus, Julie. Okay. Tell me what you saw. Everything."

Julie walked him through it, forcing herself to be methodical despite the panic rising in her chest. The signatures of famous artists. The artificial aging she'd spotted under the loupe. Wolf's recognizable technique was hidden beneath the false attribution. Jimmy's comment about "particular buyers."

"Julie." Dennis was quiet for a moment. "I covered a story once about an art fraud case in San Diego. Small-time stuff— some guy forging local artists, got caught when he tried to sell too many. But I remember some things from talking to the investigators. If what you're saying is true—if these are forg- eries meant to pass as authentic lost Impressionist works— that's serious federal territory."

"Federal?"

"FBI handles major art fraud. And Julie, if those paintings were convincing enough to fool collectors, they could be worth hundreds of thousands each. Maybe more. Impressionist paintings from that era, if they were real? We're talking museum-level valuations."

Julie felt the room tilt slightly. She walked to the window, phone cord stretching behind her. Outside, everything looked normal—palm trees, parked cars, a neighbor watering his lawn. How could the world look so ordinary when she'd just discovered something like this?

"But why would Di Nuccio accept paintings worth that much to settle a forty-thousand-dollar debt?"

"He wouldn't." Dennis was quiet, thinking. "Unless...

Julie, what if the debt was never the point? What if this was about moving the paintings through you? Think about it—you inherit them from your mother's estate, you have documentation that they came from her collection. You're paying off her debt. It gives the paintings a clean history. 'Recently surfaced from a private California collection.' That's provenance. That's what makes forgeries sellable."

Julie pressed her forehead against the cool glass. "Oh God. He used me."

"Do you still have the photos you took?"

Julie looked at the two Polaroids on her coffee table, already fading slightly in the afternoon light. "Two of them. He arrived before I could finish. And Dennis, they're just Polaroids—they're grainy, they won't show the details clearly enough for real evidence."

"But they're something. They show what you saw when you saw it. That matters." Dennis paused. "Julie, I don't know enough about this. We need to talk to someone who handles art crime. That might be the FBI, might be local police first— honestly, I don't know the protocol. But we need to talk to someone official."

"What if I'm wrong?" Julie's voice came out smaller than she intended. "What if there's some explanation I don't understand? What if I ruin Wolf's life over a mistake?"

"Then we figure that out. But Julie—if you're right, Di Nuccio just used you to help launder millions of dollars in forged artwork. And Wolf..." He trailed off.

"What about Wolf?"

Dennis took a breath. "If he created these paintings knowing they'd be sold as authentic lost masterpieces... Julie, that's not just copying paintings. That's deliberately defrauding collectors. That's conspiracy to commit fraud. That's serious criminal stuff."

Julie sank onto the couch. She thought about the year she'd known Wolf, all those patient lessons. The way he'd encouraged her interest in art, never condescending, always generous with his knowledge. And all that time—what? Had he been planning this? Had Amelia forced him into it? Was he as trapped as Julie felt now?

"I learned from him, Dennis. He was kind. And all that time…"

"You don't know what all that time was," Dennis said gently. "Maybe he was trapped. Maybe Amelia forced him somehow. You can't know until someone investigates properly."

"What do I do?"

"First, put those photos somewhere safe. Not in your house —maybe a safety deposit box at your bank? Tomorrow. Then I'm going to make some calls, see if I can track down that FBI agent from the San Diego case, or at least figure out what the protocol is for reporting something like this." He paused. "And Julie? Until we know what we're dealing with, be careful. If Di Nuccio is running a forgery operation and he thinks you suspect something…"

He didn't finish the sentence. He didn't need to. Julie remembered Jimmy's eyes watching her face as he mentioned Di Nuccio's "particular buyers."

"Okay," she whispered.

"I'll call you tomorrow. Lock your doors tonight."

After hanging up, Julie sat in the quiet living room as the afternoon light shifted, growing longer and more golden. She looked at the Polaroids on her coffee table—two grainy images that might be evidence of federal crimes, or might be worthless as proof. She thought about Wolf's hands guiding her brush, teaching her to see. She thought about Amelia's careful comments about provenance and lost paintings.

Had her mother been a criminal? A victim? Both?

Julie picked up the Polaroids and looked at them one more time. In the grainy images, she could just make out the signatures, the too-perfect craquelure, the brushwork she'd learned to recognize.

Tomorrow, she'd put them in a safety deposit box. Tomorrow, she'd wait for Dennis to call with information about who to contact. Tomorrow she'd decide whether to try talking to Wolf first, to understand his side before turning him over to federal investigators.

Tonight, she would sleep with her doors locked and wonder whether Vincent Di Nuccio already knew she'd figured something out. Whether forty thousand dollars had ever been the real price. Whether the paintings were already being prepared for sale, complete with false provenance that included her name.

Julie set the photos face down on the table, unable to keep looking at them. She walked to the window and closed the curtains against the fading light, shutting out the ordinary world that continued outside. At the same time, hers had just collapsed into something darker and more complicated than she'd ever imagined.

She didn't have answers. She had two grainy photographs, a magnifying loupe, and the sickening certainty that she'd just helped commit a crime she was only beginning to understand.

Tomorrow would have to take care of itself.

43. NO GOING BACK

Dennis circled one photograph with his pen, muttering under his breath as he picked up the magnifying glass for the third time in ten minutes. The eight images spread across his kitchen table seemed to shift and reveal new details each time he examined them, like a puzzle that kept rearranging itself.

Julie sat beside him in the morning light streaming through his apartment windows, her face pale and drawn. She nodded, her fingers tracing the edge of one photograph with trembling precision. "I kept telling myself I was being paranoid, but the more I look at these, the more obvious it becomes. Wolf painted these to look like they were done fifty years ago."

Dennis set down the magnifying glass and reached for his notebook, pages already filled with three hours of frantic research. The crash course in art fraud had given him plenty of material, but it had also made his stomach churn with the implications. "Julie, if these are high-end forgeries meant to be sold as authentic European paintings, we're talking about potential values in the hundreds of thousands. Maybe millions for the entire operation."

"Millions?" Julie's voice was barely a whisper.

"The art market for 'lost' European works from that period is huge. Collectors pay premium prices for pieces that supposedly disappeared during the wars and are just now surfacing." Dennis flipped through his notes. "I called Professor Martinez at UC Irvine—she's an expert in art authentication. She said that sophisticated forgeries often end up in legitimate auction houses and galleries."

Julie buried her face in her hands, and when she looked up, her eyes held a devastation that went deeper than fear. "Dennis, what does this say about me? About my judgment? I lived in Amelia's world for years, trusted Wolf, and thought I understood what was happening around me. Was I really that naive, or did I just choose not to see what I didn't want to see?"

Dennis reached over and squeezed her shoulder, feeling the tension coiled there. "There was no way you could know what they were doing. You trusted people who seemed trustworthy."

"But what if I didn't want to look too closely because the truth would have been inconvenient?" Julie's voice cracked. "What if I was willfully blind because asking hard questions would have made my life more complicated?"

The pain in her voice cut through Dennis's journalistic excitement and reminded him that this wasn't just a story—it was Julie's life, her sense of identity, her trust in people she'd cared about. "You didn't know," he said firmly. "You were trying to settle a debt and get your life back. That's not your fault." But even as he said it, Dennis felt the weight of what they were dealing with. This was a federal case potentially involving interstate commerce, mail fraud, wire fraud, and conspiracy. The kind of case that could make a journalist's career or get witnesses killed if they handled it wrong. I need to make some calls," Dennis said, standing and walking to the phone. "Starting with Ray Stone."

Julie looked up sharply. "Do you think he'll believe us?"

"Ray's a good detective, and he's been burned before by missing important details. I think he'll listen." Dennis dialed the police station. "Besides, he worked on Amelia's case. He knows the players."

After three transfers, Ray's familiar voice came on the line. "Stone here."

"Ray, it's Dennis Driver. I need to talk to you about something related to the Amelia Hart case. Something big."

A pause. "Okay, but that case was closed."

"I know, but Julie has discovered what looks like a major art fraud operation connected to people involved in Amelia's life. Ray, can you meet us somewhere? This isn't a phone conversation."

"How about the Coffee Pub in thirty minutes? The one next to the post office."

"We'll be there."

Dennis hung up and turned to Julie. "Pack up those photos. We're going to need Ray's help to figure out how to handle this properly."

As Julie carefully slid the photographs back into their envelope, Dennis felt the familiar surge of adrenaline that came with a big story. But this time, it was tempered by genuine fear —not just for Julie's safety, but for what they might uncover as they pulled at the threads of Wolf's forgeries and Di Nuccio's operation.

• • •

The Coffee Pub was busy with the late morning crowd, but Ray had chosen a table outside in the Lumberyard Courtyard. He looked older than Dennis remembered, lines around his eyes deeper, but his attention was sharp as Dennis and Julie laid out their discovery.

Ray studied the photographs with the methodical care Dennis had seen him apply to crime scenes. He didn't speak for several minutes, using Julie's magnifying glass to examine details, making notes in his small pad.

"This is sophisticated work," Ray finally said. "Not some amateur trying to make a quick buck. Someone with real technical skill created these."

"Wolf Schmidt," Julie said quietly. "He painted these."

Ray set down the magnifying glass and leaned back in his chair. "Okay, here's what we're dealing with. If these are high-end forgeries meant to enter the legitimate art market, that's federal jurisdiction. Wire fraud if sales were coordinated by phone, mail fraud if anything was shipped, money laundering if proceeds were moved through financial institutions."

Dennis felt his pulse quicken. "What's the next step?"

"FBI Art Crime Team. They have agents who specialize in exactly this kind of fraud. I know someone who can get us connected to the right people."

Julie looked stricken. "Ray, what if I'm wrong? What if these really are just reproductions and we're making a huge mistake?"

Ray's expression grew more serious. "Julie, the forty-thousand-dollar debt acceptance bothers me. That suggests the debt was never the real point." He leaned forward. "This feels like a laundering pipeline. Di Nuccio's 'debt collection' is just a front for acquiring art that's already been altered to pass as something valuable. You were never paying off a debt you were providing cover for moving high-end forgeries into the legitimate market."

Julie's jaw dropped.

Dennis watched her realize that she hadn't just been an unwitting accomplice—she'd been a carefully selected tool in a sophisticated criminal operation.

"What does this mean for Julie's safety?" Dennis asked, though he dreaded the answer.

"It means she needs to be very careful until we know more about the scope of this operation," Ray said bluntly. "If Di Nuccio is running a sophisticated art fraud scheme, he's not going to want witnesses talking to federal agents."

Ray turned to Dennis with a calculating look. "And you need to think about your own exposure here. You're a journalist, you're visible in the community, and you're asking questions. If Di Nuccio sees you as a threat, you could be a target too."

Dennis felt a chill run down his spine, but when he looked at Julie—pale, frightened, but resolute—his choice was clear. "I'm not backing down. Julie needs support, and this story needs to be told."

Ray nodded with what looked like approval. "Just be smart about it. Don't go anywhere alone, don't follow up on leads without backup, and assume someone might be watching."

The weight of that statement settled over the table. Dennis reached over and took Julie's hand, feeling her trembling slightly.

"What do we do now?" Dennis asked.

"Agent Sarah Chen with the FBI Art Crime Team worked a case similar to this about two years ago. If anyone can tell us how to proceed, it's her."

Dennis watched Ray make the call from the phone booth

outside the coffee shop. As he talked, Dennis caught Julie's eye and saw his own mixture of fear and determination reflected there.

They were no longer just trying to understand what had happened. They were about to become active participants in bringing down what could be a major criminal enterprise. And Dennis realized that his relationship with Julie—which had started as a professional interest and grown into something much deeper—was about to be tested by circumstances that could put them both in real danger.

Ray hung up the phone and looked at them both seriously. "Agent Chen wants to meet with us this afternoon. She's driving down from Los Angeles." He paused. "Once we take this step, there's no going back. Are you both sure you're ready for this?"

Dennis looked at Julie, seeing her jaw set with the same determination that had gotten her through months of police investigation and legal complications.

"We're ready," Julie said firmly.

Dennis squeezed her hand. "Then let's do this."

But as they gathered their materials and prepared to leave the coffee shop, Dennis couldn't shake the feeling that they were crossing a line into territory more dangerous than any of them fully understood. The excitement of uncovering a major story was still there, but a more primitive concern now over-shadowed it: keeping both of them alive long enough to see justice done.

44. PROVENANCE

Wolf stood at his kitchen window, watching the morning fog roll in from the Pacific, but his mind was elsewhere. The eight paintings were gone—delivered to Di Nuccio's operation yesterday by Jimmy's efficient hands. Months of meticulous work, aging techniques perfected over years, brushstrokes that mimicked the masters, all of it now moving through channels he couldn't control.

He lit another cigarette. The completion of the project should have brought relief. Instead, it felt like watching a fuse burn, too fast, to a box of dynamite he'd packed himself.

Carol emerged from the bedroom, already dressed for work at the gallery. She paused when she saw him standing motionless at the window, smoke curling around his head like a gray halo.

"You didn't sleep again," she said. It wasn't a question.

Wolf shrugged, not trusting his voice. How could he explain that every time he closed his eyes, he saw those eight paintings in his mind—not as they appeared now, aged and signed with dead men's names, but as they truly were? Forgeries. Beautiful lies that could send him to federal prison for twenty years.

The phone rang, cutting through the morning silence like a blade. Wolf's cigarette froze halfway to his lips.

"I'll get it," Carol said, but Wolf was already moving.

"No. I've got it." He snatched the receiver. "Schmidt."

"Wolf, my friend. Vincent here. How's the morning treating you?"

Di Nuccio's voice was warm, conversational, but Wolf detected something underneath—a current of excitement that made his stomach clench. "Fine, Vincent. Just fine."

"Good, good. Listen, I wanted to thank you for those beautiful pieces. Real quality work, as always. My buyers are very happy."

Buyers. Plural. Wolf gripped the phone tighter. "Already?"

"Oh, you know how it is in this business. Word gets around about authentic European pieces from that period. There's a collector in San Francisco, another in Phoenix. They appreciate fine art with proper... provenance."

The way Di Nuccio said "provenance" made Wolf's skin crawl. They both knew those paintings had no legitimate history, no chain of ownership that would withstand serious scrutiny. Their provenance was Wolf's skill and Di Nuccio's forgery connections—nothing more.

"Wolf? You still there?"

"Yes. I'm here."

"Excellent. Because I have another opportunity for us. Similar work, similar period. A collector in New York is looking for something specific—Alpine scenes, maybe German or Austrian, from the 1920s. You think you could manage something like that?"

Wolf's mouth went dry. Another commission. Another set

of forgeries to create and worry about. Another step deeper into a hole, he was beginning to realize he might never climb out of it.

"I... when would you need them?"

"No rush. Take your time, do it right. Quality over speed, that's what separates you from the amateurs." Di Nuccio's chuckle held no warmth. "We'll talk soon, my friend."

The line went dead. Wolf stood holding the receiver until the dial tone became unbearable, then hung up slowly.

Carol was watching him from the kitchen doorway, her face creased with concern. "Wolf? What's wrong? You look like you've seen a ghost."

I am the ghost. The ghost of who I used to be. "Nothing," he said, forcing a smile. "Just business."

Carol moved closer, her eyes searching his face with an intensity that made him want to look away. "Wolf, talk to me. What's happening? Ever since Amelia died, you've been..." She searched for words. "You've been different. Scared." She paused, then asked the question that cut straight to his heart: "Is someone making you do this, Wolf?"

The directness of it nearly broke him. For a moment, he wanted to tell her how he felt trapped by Di Nuccio. But the words stuck in his throat. "I'm fine, Carol. Just tired."

She studied his face for a long moment, and Wolf saw the exact moment she decided not to push. It was a small mercy, but one that made him feel even more isolated.

"I'm going to the market," she said quietly. "I'll see you later."

• • •

After she left, Wolf walked through their house like a man surveying a crime scene. In the spare bedroom he'd converted to a home studio, evidence of his crimes lay scattered across every surface. Bottles of aging solutions—tea stains, coffee grounds, carefully mixed chemicals that could add decades to a canvas overnight. Brushes worn to match the techniques of long-dead masters. Reference books on European painting styles, filled with bookmarks and margin notes.

On the easel sat a piece he'd been working on, a German Alpine scene in the style of Heinrich Brenner, circa 1924. Wolf approached the canvas slowly, studying his own work with a critical eye that had been trained by years of deception. The technique was flawless. He'd captured Brenner's particular way of handling light on snow, his distinctive brushwork in rendering pine trees. With proper aging and the right signature, this painting could easily pass for authentic in all but the most sophisticated examinations.

And that was the problem.

Wolf's hand trembled as he picked up a palette knife. With one swift motion, he dragged it across the canvas, destroying hours of meticulous work. Paint smeared and mixed, the Alpine scene became an abstract mess of colors.

But destroying one painting couldn't undo what he'd already done. Eight forgeries were now in Di Nuccio's pipeline, about to be sold to collectors who would never suspect they were buying beautiful lies. And Di Nuccio wanted more.

Wolf sank into his painting chair, a piece of furniture that had once been his throne, the place where he created art that mattered. Now it felt like an electric chair, the place where he'd sentenced himself to a life he no longer recognized.

He thought about the early days, when Amelia had first

approached him about "restoration" work. She'd been so charming, so persuasive. "Just touching up some pieces that have been damaged over the years," she'd said. "Your technical skills are exactly what's needed."

When had "touching up" become "reproducing"? When had "reproducing" become "forging"? The progression had seemed so gradual, so reasonable at each step. A little more reconstruction here, a signature that needed to be "restored" there. Before he knew it, he was creating entirely new paintings in the styles of dead artists, aging them to perfection, signing names that weren't his own.

The worst part was how good he'd become at it. His forgeries weren't just passable—they were masterful. Museums might be fooled. Art historians could be deceived. In some twisted way, it was the finest work he'd ever done.

Wolf stubbed out his cigarette and immediately reached for another. Every time the phone rang, every unexpected knock at the door, every police siren in the distance—it all felt like the moment his carefully constructed life would come crashing down.

And now Di Nuccio wanted more.

The sound of a car door slamming in the driveway made him jump. Through the window, he saw a man in a dark suit walking toward the front door—not Jimmy, someone he didn't recognize. Wolf's heart hammered against his ribs as he waited for the knock.

When it came, it was polite but firm. Official.

Wolf approached the door slowly, his mind racing through possibilities. Police? FBI? Immigration? Some other agency he hadn't considered?

He opened the door to find a young man with an earnest face and a leather portfolio. "Mr. Schmidt? I'm David

Rodriguez with Chubb Insurance. I'm investigating some questions about authentication and provenance in the local art market. I was wondering if I could ask you a few questions about your restoration work?"

Wolf's blood turned to ice water. "I... what kind of questions?"

"Nothing too formal. We're just trying to get a better understanding of how restoration work is documented, particularly for pieces that might be entering the collector market." The man's smile was friendly, but his eyes were sharp, calculating. He pulled a small notepad from his jacket—already open to a page with a list of names. Wolf could see his own name circled in red ink.

Wolf stood frozen in the doorway, every instinct screaming at him to slam the door and run. But running would only confirm suspicions. Instead, he heard himself saying, "Of course. Come in."

As he led the investigator into his living room, Wolf noticed the man didn't look around like a curious guest. He scanned—memorizing layout, noting exit routes, cataloging details with the efficiency of someone who'd done this many times before.

Wolf realized that his nightmare had just taken a new turn. The walls were closing in, and he was running out of places to hide.

The question now was how much time he had before they found the evidence to convict him.

45. PROOF OF INTENT

Ray Stone sat in the FBI field office in Los Angeles, feeling simultaneously impressed and intimidated by the sleek efficiency around him. Federal agents moved with purpose through glass-walled conference rooms, their conversations muted but intense. The Art Crime Team occupied a corner of the floor where laminated evidence boards and UV scanning lamps gave it the look of an art historian's war room, their walls covered with photographs of stolen masterpieces and organizational charts tracking international art theft rings.

Agent Sarah Chen studied the photographs Julie had taken, her expression growing more serious with each image. She couldn't have been older than thirty-five, but her credentials were impressive: Harvard art history degree, FBI training at Quantico, five years specializing in art fraud cases that had recovered millions in stolen works.

"These are sophisticated," she said finally, setting down her magnifying glass. "Whoever created these has serious technical skill and extensive knowledge of 1920s European painting techniques."

"Wolf Schmidt," Ray said, straightening in his seat and flipping his notebook to a fresh page. "German immigrant, been in Laguna Beach for about three years. Legitimate artist but supplementing his income with forgery work."

Dennis leaned forward from his seat beside Julie. "How can you tell they're forgeries just from photographs?"

Chen smiled slightly. "Training and experience. But also, forgers always make the same mistakes." She pointed to one of the images. "See this cracking pattern? It's too uniform. Real aging happens randomly over decades— environmental factors, temperature changes, and how the painting was stored and handled. This looks like chemical aging, probably done in a controlled environment."

Julie shifted uncomfortably in her chair. "So, I definitely handed over evidence of federal crimes?"

"Most likely, yes." Chen's voice was gentle but firm. "But you're not in legal jeopardy here, Ms. Bloom. You were an unwitting participant used to launder the forgeries into the legitimate market."

Ray pulled out his pen. "What's our next step? Do we have enough for warrants?"

"Not yet," Chen said. "We need more evidence of the operation—financial records, communications between conspirators, proof of intent to defraud collectors." She looked at Ray with respect. "But your detective work on the original Amelia Hart case gives us valuable background. You understand the relationships between these people."

"I missed a lot the first time around," Ray said quietly. "I won't make those mistakes again."

"Your initial investigation was solid," Chen assured him. "Art fraud wasn't part of the murder inquiry. Now we're looking at a completely different type of crime."

She stood and walked to a whiteboard, uncapping a

marker. "Let me show you what we're dealing with." She began sketching an organizational chart. "Vincent Di Nuccio appears to be running a sophisticated art fraud operation. He uses legitimate debts—like the one to Amelia Hart—as cover for acquiring forged artwork."

"How does that work exactly?" Dennis asked, his journalist instincts engaged.

"It's brilliant, actually. A kind of legitimacy laundering. Instead of trying to smuggle fake art into galleries or auction houses directly, Di Nuccio creates scenarios where innocent parties voluntarily hand over the forgeries. Julie settling her debt looks completely legitimate on paper."

Ray studied the emerging chart. "So Di Nuccio gets a clean title to the paintings through Julie, then sells them to collectors as authentic antiques?"

"Exactly. And if questions are ever raised about authenticity, the chain of ownership leads back to a legitimate debt settlement, not a criminal conspiracy."

Julie looked stricken, then surprised herself by asking, "I'll study my mother's records for other suspicious transactions?"

Chen nodded approvingly. "That's exactly the kind of thinking we need. Yes—any documentation of other 'debt settlements' involving artwork, unusual financial transactions, communications between Amelia and Di Nuccio."

"So, I wasn't just an unwitting accomplice," Julie continued. "I was essential to the whole scheme?"

"You provided the legitimacy they needed," Chen confirmed. "But that also makes you a valuable witness. You can testify about how the operation works."

Ray leaned back in his chair, pieces clicking into place. "What about Wolf Schmidt? Is he a willing participant or another victim?"

"That's what we need to determine. If he's creating forgeries under duress, he might be willing to cooperate. If he's a full partner..." Chen shrugged. "Twenty years in federal prison."

Dennis's pen had been moving rapidly across his notepad, but now it stopped entirely. "What kind of evidence do you need to build a case?"

"Financial records showing payments between Di Nuccio and Schmidt. Communications about the forgeries—phone calls, letters, anything documenting the conspiracy. Physical evidence from Schmidt's studio showing forgery materials and techniques." Chen capped her marker. "And ideally, we'd like Schmidt to cooperate and testify against Di Nuccio. But we're working against the clock here. One of these pieces is scheduled for handoff to a collector in San Francisco tomorrow afternoon. If we miss that, it disappears into a private collection where we may never recover it."

Julie stared at the organizational chart. Dennis's pen hovered over his notepad, unmoving. Even Ray, normally steady, found himself holding his breath.

"How do we approach Schmidt?" Ray finally asked. "If we spook him, he might destroy evidence or run."

"Carefully," Chen said. "We need to assess his psychological state, figure out if he's more afraid of Di Nuccio or law enforcement." She looked at Ray thoughtfully. "You knew him through the Amelia Hart investigation. What's your read on his character?"

Ray considered. "Seemed genuinely grief-stricken about Amelia's death. Not a hardened criminal type. More like someone who got in over his head and doesn't know how to get out."

"That's our best-case scenario. Someone like that might be

willing to cooperate if we can guarantee his safety and offer a reasonable plea deal."

Julie spoke up quietly. "What about his wife, Carol? I think she might know about the forgeries."

"Another potential witness," Chen noted. "Or leverage to get Schmidt to cooperate."

Dennis looked uncomfortable. "Are we talking about threatening innocent people?"

"We're talking about offering protection to people who might be in danger," Chen corrected. "If Schmidt is working under duress, Di Nuccio won't hesitate to eliminate witnesses who could expose the operation."

The silence that followed was heavy, filled with the weight of unspoken implications about what "eliminate" might mean.

"What's the timeline?" Ray asked.

"Fast," Chen said. "If these forgeries are already moving to buyers, we need to intercept them before they disappear into private collections. Once a fake masterpiece is hanging in some collector's private study, it becomes much harder to recover."

She walked to her desk and pulled out a thick folder. "I'm opening a formal federal investigation. Ray, I'd like you to coordinate with local law enforcement. Dennis, you'll need to hold off on publishing anything until we've made arrests. We can't afford to spook the targets."

"What about surveillance?" Ray asked.

"Already in motion. We've had Di Nuccio's known associates under loose surveillance since this morning. Nothing obvious, just tracking movement and communications."

Ray felt his pulse quicken. It was the kind of complex, multi-jurisdictional case that had always excited him as a detective. But it was also exactly the kind of case where small mistakes could have huge consequences.

"Agent Chen," he said carefully, "I need to ask—what's my role here? This is your investigation, your jurisdiction."

She smiled. "You're local liaison and consultant. You know these people, you understand their relationships, and frankly, your detective skills are exactly what we need for this kind of work." She paused. "Ray, I've read your file. You're a good detective who got handed a nearly impossible case with the Hart investigation. This is your chance to help bring real criminals to justice."

"Thank you. I won't let you down."

"I know you won't." Chen turned to Julie and Dennis. "You two need to be very careful. If Di Nuccio suspects you've discovered the nature of the paintings, you could be in real danger."

Julie gripped Dennis's hand. "What should we do?"

"Normal routine, but stay alert. Don't go anywhere alone, don't meet with anyone connected to Di Nuccio, and call immediately if anything seems suspicious." Chen handed them each a card with a direct phone number. "This reaches me twenty-four hours a day."

As they prepared to leave, Ray felt the familiar weight of responsibility settling on his shoulders. But this time, it felt different—not like a burden he was carrying alone, but like part of a team effort where his experience and skills mattered.

He'd spent months second-guessing every decision he'd made in the Amelia Hart case. Now he had a chance to use those hard-learned lessons to help take down criminals who were still active, still dangerous.

"Agent Chen," he said as they reached the door, "how confident are you that we can make this case?"

She considered the question seriously. "If Schmidt cooperates, very confident. If he doesn't..." She shrugged. "We'll need to build it piece by piece. But Ray, that's what good detective work is about. Building cases that can't be torn down."

As they walked out of the federal building into the bright Los Angeles afternoon, Ray realized he felt more like a real detective than he had in months. The mistakes of the past hadn't ruined him—they'd taught him how to do better.

And this time, he was going to get it right.

46. THE FINAL BRUSH STROKE

The wire felt like a snake against Wolf's chest, the tiny microphone taped just below his collarbone where Chen had assured him it wouldn't be detected. He sat in his car outside Di Nuccio's warehouse, hands trembling as he lit what he promised himself would be his last cigarette as a free man.

Carol had cried when he told her. Not the angry tears he'd expected, but something deeper—grief for the man she'd thought she knew, relief that the lies were finally ending. "I've been waiting for you to tell me the truth for months," she'd whispered. "I knew something was destroying you."

Now, walking toward the warehouse door, Wolf felt lighter than he had in years. The weight of deception, of living a lie, of compromising everything he'd once believed about art and integrity—all of it was finally lifting.

"Wolf, my friend!" Di Nuccio's voice boomed across the warehouse as Wolf entered. "Perfect timing. I've got buyers lined up for your Alpine pieces, and I have another commission that's going to make us both very wealthy."

Wolf forced a smile, knowing that Agent Chen and her

team were listening to every word through the transmitter hidden in his jacket. "What kind of commission, Vincent?"

"Big money this time. A collector in New York wants a complete series—six paintings, all French Impressionist style, circa 1890s. He's willing to pay two million for authentic pieces from that period." Di Nuccio's eyes gleamed with greed. "Of course, we both know they won't be authentic, but they'll be perfect. Your work always is."

"Two million," Wolf repeated, making sure the wire picked up the amount clearly. "And he believes he's buying genuine Impressionist works?"

"He'll never know the difference. Not with your skills." Di Nuccio clapped Wolf on the shoulder. "We've built something beautiful here, Wolf. A perfect system. Legitimate ownership transfers, undetectable forgeries, wealthy collectors who get exactly what they want to see. Everyone wins."

Wolf nodded, his stomach churning at Di Nuccio's casual attitude toward massive fraud. "What about the eight land-scapes from Amelia's debt? Have those found buyers?"

"Three sold already. The Loire Valley piece went to a collector in Phoenix for four hundred thousand. The German village scene is heading to a private gallery in San Francisco tomorrow." Di Nuccio pulled out a folder filled with docu-ments. "Clean provenance, all legitimate sales on paper. No one will ever trace them back to us."

Wolf stared at the folder, knowing that Chen now had enough evidence to charge Di Nuccio with multiple federal crimes. Wire fraud, mail fraud, money laundering— the works.

"Vincent," Wolf said carefully, "what happens if someone questions the authenticity? If an expert realizes they're forgeries?"

Di Nuccio's expression darkened slightly. "That's why we're careful about our buyers, Wolf. We sell to people who want to believe, who don't ask too many questions. And if someone does get suspicious..." He shrugged. "Well, we make sure they understand the benefits of keeping quiet."

The implied threat hung in the air like smoke. Wolf felt sweat beading on his forehead despite the warehouse's cool temperature.

Di Nuccio's gaze lingered on Wolf just a moment too long. "You sure you're alright, my friend? You seem...

different today. Nervous, maybe?"

Wolf's heart hammered against the wire taped to his chest. "Just thinking about the risks, Vincent. Two million dollars is a lot of money. A lot of attention if something goes wrong."

"Nothing's going to go wrong," Di Nuccio said, but his eyes remained suspicious. "We've been doing this for months without a problem. You're not getting cold feet on me, are you, Wolf?"

"No, of course not." Wolf forced himself to meet Di Nuccio's stare. "I just want to make sure we're being careful."

Di Nuccio studied him for another long moment, then seemed to relax. "Good. Because we've got a beautiful future ahead of us, my friend. More commissions than we can handle, buyers with deep pockets, and a foolproof system." He smiled. "Just keep creating those masterpieces, and I'll keep finding people willing to pay premium prices for lost European treasures."

Wolf nodded, knowing that this conversation had just sealed Di Nuccio's fate—and his own. In fifteen minutes, federal agents would swarm this warehouse. Di Nuccio would be in handcuffs, and Wolf would begin the long process of paying for his crimes.

But for the first time in months, Wolf felt like himself again.

R ay Stone coordinated the federal operation from a command vehicle parked three blocks from Di Nuccio's warehouse, radio chatter crackling around him as Agent Chen's team moved into position. Six months ago, he'd been a detective who'd missed crucial evidence in a murder case. Today, he was helping to take down a multi-million-dollar art fraud operation.

"Alpha team in position at the warehouse," came the voice through his headset.

"Beta team covering the rear exit," another agent reported.

"Gamma team standing by at Schmidt's residence."

Agent Chen sat beside Ray, monitoring Wolf's wire transmission through high-tech equipment that made Ray's police radio look like a toy. The German artist's voice came through clearly, along with Di Nuccio's incriminating admissions about forged masterpieces and intimidating suspicious buyers.

"Two million for six fake Impressionist paintings," Chen murmured, making notes. "We've got enough to put Di Nuccio away for twenty years."

Ray felt the familiar tension of an operation about to go live. But this time, it was different. Instead of working alone, trying to piece together a puzzle with missing pieces, he was part of a coordinated team with clear objectives and overwhelming resources.

"Schmidt's getting nervous," Chen said, listening to Wolf's increasingly strained conversation with Di Nuccio. "Di Nuccio's suspicious."

"Wolf can handle it," Ray said. "He's got more courage than he knows."

"Wait. Di Nuccio's moving toward the back of the warehouse. He might be getting ready to run." Agent Chen pressed her earpiece. "All teams, target may be attempting to flee. Prepare for immediate entry."

Ray watched through binoculars as federal agents adjusted their positions around the warehouse. The careful choreography of the takedown suddenly felt more urgent, more dangerous.

"Schmidt's still in there," Chen announced. "Di Nuccio's showing him something—looks like more forged pieces. We're getting everything on tape."

She keyed her radio. "All teams, we are go. Execute, execute, execute."

Ray watched the takedown unfold with professional appreciation. Federal agents moved with precision and overwhelming force. Di Nuccio barely had time to register what was happening before he was face-down on the warehouse floor, hands zip-tied behind his back.

Within minutes, Wolf was being processed as a cooperating witness, and agents were cataloging evidence that would support dozens of federal charges.

"Beautiful work," Ray said to Agent Chen as they watched the warehouse operation conclude.

"Couldn't have happened without your local knowledge and Wolf's cooperation," she replied. "You should be proud, Ray. This is what good detective work looks like."

Ray felt something shift inside him—a knot of self-doubt and professional insecurity that had been there since the Hart case finally loosened. He hadn't failed as a detective. He'd learned, grown, and contributed to real justice.

His radio crackled. "Detective Stone, we've recovered forty-three forged artworks, financial records documenting over three million in fraudulent sales, and enough evidence to dismantle Di Nuccio's entire operation."

Ray smiled, keying his radio. "Copy that. Good work, everyone."

For the first time in months, Ray Stone felt like the detective he'd always wanted to be

J ulie sat in the federal building's witness interview room, her hands folded in her lap as Agent Chen reviewed her statement one final time. Through the window, she could see Dennis in the hallway, waiting for her testimony to conclude.

"Ms. Bloom, your cooperation has been essential to this case," Chen said. "Your photos cracked the case. Your story made it undeniable."

Julie nodded, still processing the scope of what she'd unknowingly participated in. "How much were those eight paintings really worth?"

"If they'd been sold as authentic European masterpieces? Probably two to three million dollars total." Agent Chen closed her folder. "Di Nuccio didn't accept them to settle a forty-thousand-dollar debt. He acquired them because they were worth fifty times that much."

The numbers were staggering. Julie thought about her months of worry over the debt, her fear of losing her house, her desperate relief when Di Nuccio had agreed to the art settlement. She'd been a pawn in a game whose stakes she'd never understood.

"What about Amelia?" Julie asked quietly. "How much did she know?"

Agent Chen's expression softened. "From what Wolf

Schmidt has told us, Amelia was manipulated by Di Nuccio just like you were. She thought she was commissioning legitimate reproductions for her personal collection. Di Nuccio convinced her to use Wolf's skills for 'restoration' work, then gradually drew both of them into the forgery operation."

Julie felt a wave of relief mixed with sadness. Amelia hadn't been a criminal mastermind—she'd been another victim of Di Nuccio's manipulation, someone whose love of art had been exploited by a sophisticated con man.

"So she died not knowing what she'd gotten involved in?"

"We believe so. Wolf says she became suspicious toward the end, started asking questions about where the 'restored' pieces were going. Di Nuccio may have been planning to cut her out of the operation entirely."

Julie closed her eyes, imagining Amelia's final months. She probably realized she'd been deceived and was trying to find a way out of the situation. It made her accidental death even more tragic.

"What happens now?" Julie asked.

"Di Nuccio will face federal charges that could result in twenty to thirty years in prison. Wolf Schmidt will likely receive a reduced sentence in exchange for his cooperation. The forged artworks will be catalogued as evidence and eventually destroyed."

Julie thought about Wolf, remembering his gentle manner and obvious skill as an artist. Prison would be hard for someone like him, but at least he'd chosen to tell the truth in the end.

Agent Chen stood, extending her hand to Julie. "Thank you again for your cooperation. This case couldn't have been made without citizens like you who are willing to do the right thing."

As Julie shook the agent's hand, she realized something

had fundamentally changed in how she saw herself. She was no longer just someone things happened to. She was someone who could make things happen, who could choose justice over convenience, truth over comfort.

Walking out to meet Dennis in the hallway, Julie felt a sense of closure she hadn't expected. The art fraud case was over, Di Nuccio would face justice, and she'd played a role in making that happen.

"How do you feel?" Dennis asked, taking her hand as they walked toward the elevator.

Julie considered the question. "Free," she said finally. "Really free, for the first time since my mother died."

T HE END

EPILOGUE

Six Months Later

W olf Schmidt sat in the federal prison library, working on a legitimate painting for the first time in years. The subject was simple—a view of the mountains visible through the barred window—but every brushstroke felt honest, authentic, his own.

Carol visited every week, bringing news from the outside world and encouragement for his appeals process. Agent Chen had recommended a reduced sentence based on his cooperation, but Wolf's first parole hearing had been denied. He was learning to measure hope in smaller increments.

Ray Stone received a commendation from the FBI Art Crime Team and a promotion within the Laguna Beach Police Department. More importantly, he'd regained confidence in his abilities as a detective, applying the lessons from the Hart case to new investigations with patience and thoroughness.

Julie and Dennis were planning their wedding, to be held in the garden of the house Julie had fought so hard to keep. She'd turned Amelia's gallery into a legitimate operation focused on supporting local artists, though she still sometimes wondered about the pieces in Amelia's collection that had never been fully authenticated.

Vincent Di Nuccio was sentenced to twenty-five years in federal prison on multiple counts of wire fraud, mail fraud, money laundering, and racketeering. The millions in assets seized from his operation were used to compensate defrauded collectors and fund art crime prevention programs.

One painting, however, had vanished before the arrests— the Loire Valley landscape that had been scheduled for delivery to San Francisco. Agent Chen suspected it had already crossed into Europe, beyond the reach of American law enforcement, but not beyond her memory. Some cases, she'd learned, never truly close.

The art fraud case was officially resolved, but its lessons continued to resonate that truth, however painful, was always preferable to beautiful lies; that justice required ordinary people to make extraordinary choices; and that redemption was possible for those brave enough to face the consequences of their actions.

In the end, the most valuable thing recovered wasn't forged masterpieces worth millions of dollars—it was the integrity of people who chose to do the right thing, even when it cost them everything they thought they wanted.

ALSO BY PHILLIP DAIGLE

Tides of Acadia

In the early 17th century, the wild, untamed lands of Acadia— now
the Maritime Provinces of Canada—were a contested territory
between the French and the English, and the Mi'kmaq people who
inhabited the region. Amidst this turbulent time, three individuals
stand out: Charles La Tour, Francoise Jacquelin, and Menou Daulnay.
Their stories intertwine in a complex web of loyalty, love, and
betrayal in the historical drama Tides of Acadia.

The Acadian

Olivier, an indentured servant from France, finds himself in Acadia.
Craving the thrill of the fur trade, he escapes his master's control. His
life takes a sharp turn when he observes a brutal act carried out by
renegade English soldiers. Influenced by Atahocam, a Mi'kmaw
warrior seeking vengeance for his murdered family, Olivier becomes
embroiled in the ensuing conflict.

www.phillipdaigle.com

ABOUT THE AUTHOR

Philip Daigle is an American mystery and historical fiction author best known for his novels "Canvas of Secrets, "Tides of Acadia" and "The Acadian." His storytelling, rich in historical detail, draws readers into the vivid past, offering immersive narratives that speak to the struggles and triumphs of its people. Philip's commitment to historical fiction is a testament to his love for history and skill in crafting compelling, character-driven stories that reanimate the past for modern readers.

www.phillipdaigle.com